MARRY KILL

ABOUT THE AUTHOR

Yemi Dipeolu is a British-Nigerian writer from South East London. She studied English Literature with Creative Writing at the University of Surrey and has an MFA from Kingston University. *Kiss Marry Kill* is her first novel.

KISS
MARRY
KILL

YEMI DIPEOLU

faber

First published in the UK in 2026
by Faber & Faber Ltd
The Bindery, 51 Hatton Garden
London EC1N 8HN

Typeset by Typo•glyphix, Burton-on-Trent DE14 3HE
Printed and bound in the UK by CPI Group (UK) Ltd, Croydon CR0 4YY

All rights reserved
© Yemi Dipeolu, 2026

The right of Yemi Dipeolu to be identified as author of this work
has been asserted in accordance with Section 77 of the
Copyright, Designs and Patents Act 1988

*This is a work of fiction. Names, characters, places and incidents are
products of the author's imagination or are used fictitiously and are
not to be construed as real. Any resemblance to actual events, locales,
organisations or persons, living or dead, is entirely coincidental*

A CIP record for this book
is available from the British Library

ISBN 978–0–571–39586–6

Printed and bound in the UK on FSC® certified paper in line with our continuing
commitment to ethical business practices, sustainability and the environment.
For further information see faber.co.uk/environmental-policy

Our authorised representative in the EU for product safety is
Easy Access System Europe, Mustamäe tee 50, 10621 Tallinn, Estonia
gpsr.requests@easproject.com

2 4 6 8 10 9 7 5 3 1

FOR MK

PROLOGUE

Ade watches as she walks towards him, her dress skimming the floor as she moves, her face shielded by a veil. He knows that underneath it she is beautiful, that beneath her flowing dress she is carrying something even more beautiful than herself.

He sees this, acknowledges it, but he does not feel it. His spirit does not dance at the sight of her, his eyes do not fill with joyous tears at the prospect of starting a family with her.

He knows that he is selfish, that he is being selfish marrying her, but he wonders too what kind of woman would sign up for a life like this?

A woman who loves you, she had claimed once when he'd had the audacity to ask. Ade had not believed her. Even now as he stands at the altar, he still does not believe her. Could love really accept that it cannot be loved back but love anyway? Would love really risk its own destruction so that it could try to heal another, far too broken to be fixed?

If it can, then it is exactly the kind of love that Ade needs, for although he does not love her, she has become his oxygen: the thing he needs to keep from drowning.

And so, here he stands, heart not racing, nerves as still as a summer's day, just wishing he could walk away. But he can't. He cannot let his family down.

His mother, who is sobbing in the front row, her garishly tied gele nearly reaching the sky as if it too were rejoicing, relieved that her son is finally getting married, that he is finally over Cynthia, the 'Jamo girl', would never forgive him if he fled.

And so, Ade says *I do* and plants a soft passionless kiss on his new wife's lips.

At the reception, he pretends to enjoy himself.

He obliges when she asks him to dance. Accepts the spray of pounds and naira, tokens of well wishes in their new life.

Later, when the Guinness has flowed and the jollof has been eaten, Ade sees her, his Cynthia, hiding in plain sight. Amongst the colourful masses, she is wearing black, her skin glistening under the warm romantic lights, her eyes, full of malice, locked in on his.

He wants to rush towards her, to tell her that what she's seeing here means nothing, but when he rises to his feet, interrupting his brother Tayo's speech as he does so, the only word he can form is her name, which after so long feels foreign on his lips. His brother falls silent, and the rest of the crowd turn their heads in the direction Ade is looking. Seeing nothing, they turn back, their faces the perfect picture of confusion and concern.

Ade nearly crashes into the cake trying to get to her. The cake topper shakes threateningly from side to side before finally toppling over. It is too late, though. She moves too quickly, or he moves too slowly. She is gone, through the door, before he has a chance to call her name again.

The grief he's spent the past three months trying to suppress at last overwhelms him, and before he knows it he is on the floor crying, on his knees begging. It is because of this that Ade does not hear the door opening, or his mother shouting that this is the wedding of two respectable families, that they have no business being here. It is only when two pairs of arms drag him up by his armpits, when one pair of those arms pushes his hands behind his back and forces him into a more tangible form of captivity, that he realises what's going on.

You're under arrest on suspicion of murder.

The rest is a blur. His brother rushes to his side, his mother clings to his ankles crying 'Omo mi, Omo mi o . . .'

Ade pays them no mind. He allows the police officers to pull him away, and the entire wedding party follows them out of the hall and onto the street.

The wife he doesn't want but desperately needs is standing quite apart from everyone else, her hands resting on her tummy.

For the first time that day, Ade lets his gaze meet hers, and he finds, just as he'd expected, that unmoving look of desperation.

He gives her a small smile as the squad car skirts away from the pavement and into the dark Dorset road.

CHAPTER ONE

Twelve weeks before Cynthia's disappearance

It was an unusually hot spring evening and the stifling air sizzled with warning. As Cynthia Bennet sped down the M3, she did her best to ignore the feeling of mounting panic in her chest.

Breathe, she told herself, closing the window in an attempt to convince herself that it was the gentle breeze making the hairs on her arms stand up.

With a sigh, Cynthia glanced over at Ade, her partner of three years, who'd been staring at her for the better part of five minutes.

'I don't know what you want me to say,' she told him, indicating left so she could merge into the slip road. 'I get why you didn't want to tell her, but why did you have to drop this on me now?'

'I'm sorry,' he said, for what felt like the hundredth time since his announcement. 'I just didn't want you to have to lie too.'

Which was exactly how it was going to look anyway.

When Ade finally told his mother that they'd moved from London to Dorset over a year ago without telling her, Cynthia was sure she'd be accused of using her so-called feminine wiles to lure him into a life of deception. Sure, Ade would admit that it had all been his idea, but that would only serve to amplify his mother's disdain for her, which Ade claimed she was imagining. Apparently, his mother's snide comments and backhanded compliments were her way of showing affection.

'So, what do you want me to do?' Cynthia asked, turning her attention back to the road. They were in the city now, and, as she took in the tall shiny buildings looming over dilapidated storefronts, she was momentarily distracted by how much London had changed since they'd moved away.

She'd grown up in Manchester, and the city, whichever one, had always been the place she felt most at home. She had never considered that after only a year away the never-ending rows of traffic would surprise her, or that the group of schoolgirls, their skirts hiked up well above their knees, their enormous Primark earrings dazzling in the sunlight, would no longer remind her of herself.

Ade had occasionally spoken of his desire to someday leave the city life behind and live somewhere where the houses were separated by more than a single wall, but at the time Cynthia hadn't taken him seriously. She'd thought that, like her, he'd be miserable anywhere else. But then he'd found their cottage in Windchapel, with its white-bricked fireplace and wood-panelled ceilings, and before she knew it they were spending their Saturdays looking up kitchen designs on Pinterest.

'Nothing,' Ade replied. 'You don't have to do anything.'

'So, you *do* want me to lie.'

'No.' He slipped his hand onto her knee and stroked it with his thumb in a way he knew she liked.

'I'll tell her soon, I promise,' Ade said. 'We just really need tonight to go well. And if we bring it up . . .'

'Fine,' Cynthia relented, even though she didn't feel fine at all. This was the first time Mama had invited her to dinner without Ade's interference, and she'd never felt so nervous in her life. The fact that she now had to lie to Mama's face only intensified her anxiety.

'Music?' Ade asked, changing the subject as Cynthia slowed for a red light. They watched in silence as an elderly woman pushed an empty pram to the other side of the street.

'And babe . . .' Ade said, the sound of Boyz II Men crooning about some unidentified misdeed filling the car.

'Yeah, I know.' Cynthia rolled her eyes. 'You're sorry.'

Half an hour later, Cynthia was on the floor, looking up at Mama.

Both her knees were touching the ground, and she flicked her eyes to Ade, who gave her an encouraging nod, reassuring her that she was greeting Mama correctly – unlike last time.

Mama, meanwhile, was observing her with a tight-lipped smile that didn't even try to reach her eyes. Her carefully shaped eyebrows were raised, and Cynthia couldn't tell if she was annoyed or impressed. It bothered her, how much she wanted Mama's approval, how desperately she wanted to get this right.

A few long, silent seconds passed before Mama spoke.

'Please, my dear,' she said, and to Cynthia's surprise she reached out a hand to pull her up. 'I know you *Jamaicans* don't kneel in your culture. There is no need to pretend here. Come,' she added, glancing up at Ade, who at six-two was almost a foot taller than both Cynthia and Mama. 'Your brother is waiting.'

Inside, Ade's younger brother, Tayo, was already seated at the table, which was adorned with a red-and-white tablecloth. A candlelit centrepiece cast a warm light over the expensive-looking crockery stacked next to it. It all felt strangely romantic.

'See, I told you she liked you,' Ade whispered. 'She doesn't bring out the dolphin centrepiece for just anyone, trust me.'

He led her into the dining room where he took his seat at the head of the table. Mama claimed the seat to Ade's right, but when Cynthia tried to sit to his left, Mama rushed to her side and dragged the chair away from her.

'That chair is rickety,' she announced, rocking it from

side to side to emphasise her point. 'Why don't you go and sit next to Tayo over there.' She pointed to the seat at the far end of the table, closest to the door. Resisting the urge to test the chair herself, Cynthia slipped into the seat next to Tayo. Mama glanced at the clock on the wall and tutted.

'Welcome to the reject zone,' Tayo whispered, and even though he'd meant it as a joke, Cynthia felt for him. At the few family events Cynthia had been to, Tayo had been on the receiving end of Mama's fiery tongue, and his relationship with Ade seemed distant at best. She'd asked him about it once, and he'd tried to shrug it off. He was clearly the outcast of the family, a position Cynthia understood far too well, and they'd become fast friends. He'd told her about how much he wanted to drop out of medical school to study design, and she'd shared photos of the small boat she'd bought, which he teased her endlessly about. She realised now that Tayo also hadn't told Mama about her and Ade moving to Windchapel, and she wondered if he'd known that Ade had been keeping it a secret.

'In Jesus' name,' Mama said, and everyone bowed their heads while Mama blessed the food and cursed 'any known or unknown enemy who dared threaten the happiness of her family'. Tayo snorted, and opened one eye to look at Cynthia, which made her feel a little better.

After Mama concluded her prayer, the family passed around the plates, and then the Pyrex dishes filled with the

Nigerian food Cynthia was only just beginning to learn about. Jollof rice was scooped onto plates, efo and pounded yam expertly dished out.

'Babe?' Ade held up the dish in his hand, and Cynthia suddenly felt like she was on trial, the meal she chose acting as evidence of her guilt or innocence.

If she had what Ade was having, Mama might see it as a sign of weakness, like she didn't have a mind of her own, but she didn't want to risk eating Mama's jollof rice either. It had not agreed with her last time.

In the end, Cynthia settled on some plantain with a few pieces of chicken – not much, but at least she knew she could finish it.

Mama eyed Cynthia's half-empty plate and looked as if she was about to say something when the doorbell rang. The group turned their attention to Mama. They weren't expecting anyone else.

'Oh,' Mama said, patting her hair as she stood. 'Please excuse me.' As she ambled off to answer the door, the remaining trio exchanged confused glances.

A few moments later, Mama returned to the dining room, a tall woman dressed in a navy-blue skirt suit and high-heeled shoes following behind her. Her face was carefully made up – dark-red lipstick had been expertly applied, and long straight hair fell neatly over her shoulders.

Cynthia could immediately tell that it was her real hair

and not a weave, and she brushed the already slick edges of her own Afro puff with her hands, suddenly feeling uncomfortable.

'Fey-Fey?' Ade leapt from his chair, his eyes and mouth widening into a smile.

'Dey-Dey.' The woman opened her perfectly sculpted arms to greet him. He accepted her embrace, the pair swinging from side to side as they hugged, Mama standing triumphantly behind them.

Cynthia looked from Mama to Ade's back to Mama again. It didn't take a genius to figure out what Mama was up to, but if she was going to make it through this dinner with her dignity intact, she was going to have to play it cool. She refused to fall into Mama's trap, even if Ade was too blind to see the truth.

The woman turned to greet the rest of the dinner party.

'Tayo.' She smiled at Ade's brother and leant over Cynthia to give his hand a friendly squeeze. 'And . . .' Her dark-brown eyes settled on Cynthia's, and she smiled at her too, extended her hand. 'I'm Ifelayo,' she said. 'But everyone calls me Ife.'

'This is Cynthia,' Ade said, excited to introduce them. 'Cynth, you remember I told you about my friend, Ife? The one I grew up with?'

'Yeah,' Cynthia lied, smiling through gritted teeth. Ade definitely hadn't mentioned this beautiful woman he'd probably taken baths with, but Mama was smirking, and Cynthia didn't want her to think she'd won. 'Great to finally meet you.'

Ade made his way back to his chair, and Mama gestured to the seat to his left, allowing Ife to sit comfortably in the chair that didn't rickett.

'Would you like something to eat?' Mama asked.

'The efo looks lovely as always, aunty.' She said efo as if she'd come out of the womb being able to pronounce it, shortening the 'o' sound in a way Cynthia could never quite manage. No matter how many times Ade tried to teach her, she always ended up pronouncing it like 'a foe'. She looked down at her pathetically empty plate and wished she'd had the guts to try something else.

Ade pulled the Pyrex dish towards him and served Ife's food as Cynthia shrunk down further in her seat, the anxiety she'd been feeling earlier flooding back in. She'd never thought of herself as a jealous person, but the fact that this whole scenario had been choreographed by Mama had caused her usually solid self-esteem to take an unexpected nosedive. It didn't help that Ife was an absolute stunner.

'It's been way too long, Fey,' Ade said between mouthfuls. 'Where've you been?'

'Dubai, mostly. I moved back home a couple of weeks ago.'

'Your aunty tells me you were a project manager over there,' Mama said.

Ife nodded.

'We thank God.' Mama glanced over at Cynthia, cracking her chicken bone between her teeth before returning her attention back to Ife. 'There are some women in this world that think that shaking their nyash is a right way to make a living. But you, Ife, you've always been a good girl. Hard-working, respectful. You should be proud.'

Cynthia shifted in her seat. If Mama's intention was to upset her, then she'd failed. She wasn't upset; she was furious. Sure, she *shook her nyash* for a living, but so fucking what? She'd danced for some of the biggest names in the UK and had recently opened her own studio. Yes, it was small and having some serious growing pains, but it was hers, and she wasn't going to let Mama or anyone else make her feel ashamed of something she'd quite literally bled for.

Cynthia had always wondered if her career choice was behind Mama's disdain for her, but Ade had insisted that his mother didn't care about things like that. 'She only cares about what's in here,' he'd said, leaning over to touch her chest the night after she'd first met Mama.

Bullshit.

She shot Ade an 'I told you so' look, and he gave her a sad smile and a sympathetic shrug. Apparently, it was too much trouble for him to stand up for her just this once. Still, Cynthia was determined not to let Mama get to her, and she leant forward to start a conversation with *Fey-Fey.*

'What kind of projects were you working on in Dubai?' she asked, even though the conversation had already moved on.

Ife gave her a warm smile.

'Tech, mostly. I worked with a few start-ups out there which was pretty intense.'

'And now?'

'Things are quieter,' Ife replied, looking away.

'Hey,' Ade poked her with his elbow. 'Everything okay?' Ife tilted her head to look at him, and it was obvious, even to Cynthia, that everything was not. Ade said something only Ife could hear, and Ife nodded.

'Later,' she said.

'So, tell us more about Dubai,' Ade said, allowing the rest of the group back into the conversation. 'I would have killed to design some houses over there.'

'You mean back when you actually got your hands dirty.' Ife raised her eyebrows at him.

'Haha, very funny.'

Ife took a sip of the wine Cynthia had brought, the wine that Ade had told her was Mama's favourite brand and which Mama was yet to touch.

'Remember back in school when you used to draw those pictures of your dream house? The buildings over there were actually pretty similar.'

It was Ade's turn to raise his eyebrows. 'Don't tell me you still have them.'

Ife shrugged.

'I beg you burn them.'

'No way.' Ife laughed. 'They might be worth something one day.'

The conversation segued into a discussion about Ade and Ife's childhood, the games they used to play, the trouble they used to get into, etcetera etcetera, blah blah blah. It felt like they were speaking in code, shorthand forged by decades of friendship, and Cynthia gave up on trying to join in. Instead, she picked at her cold chicken and peeked at what Tayo was doing on his phone. He didn't understand their secret language either.

Eventually, she got fed up of waiting and began clearing her and Tayo's plates away in the hope that it would speed things up.

'Do you remember . . . ' Mama said, weaving her way into Ade and Ife's bantering, 'when the two of you used to play husband and wife during the summer holidays?'

Cynthia's fork fell to the ground, its clang punctuating the silence descending on the table.

'You remember, abi?' Mama continued. 'You would put on my slippers, tie a doll on your back with one of my wrappers and take Ade his Pepsi while he played that nonsense fighting game on the television.'

Ife nodded. Her eyes briefly connected with Cynthia's before she quickly looked away. 'But that was ages ago. We were just kids back then.' Her soft voice, so different from the carefree tone she'd adopted earlier, felt like someone was driving shards of broken glass into Cynthia's chest.

'Well, children know about these things deep down . . . "out of the mouth of babes", as the good book says, abi? Or am I wrong? Are you seeing anyone?'

'No, aunty, but—'

'Eh heh.' Mama clapped her hands. 'Then what are the two of you waiting for then? It's time to stop running around and settle down—'

'Mum, come on.' Tayo, not Ade, jumped to Cynthia's defence.

'Will you keep quiet there,' Mama snapped. 'Tell me if anything I have said here is a lie. Or is it too much to want my eldest son to marry a respectable Nigerian girl?'

Cynthia was shaking uncontrollably now. She knew Mama wasn't one for subtlety, but this was too far even for her. She'd spent the entire evening exercising patience, ignoring Mama's jabs to avoid causing a scene, but now her anger was finally bubbling over, and her chair fell to the ground as she shot to her feet, her vision blurry.

'Ade,' she said, pulling her bag onto her shoulder, indicating that she was ready to leave.

Ade was frozen in his seat, his mouth wide, his eyes unmoving – doing nothing, saying nothing – and in that moment Cynthia realised that she'd sadly, shamefully, fallen in love with a coward. She narrowed her eyes at him. If he was too chicken to speak up, she was going to have to do it for him.

'Ade,' Cynthia said, waving her hand in front of his face. 'We need to leave now if we don't want to get stuck on the motorway.'

'Motorway, ke?' Mama looked so genuinely shocked that Cynthia almost felt bad for her. Almost. 'Is it not just Norwood you are going to?'

Ade shifted in his seat. He gave Cynthia a barely perceptible shake of the head, his eyes begging her not to say anything.

'No, Mama,' she replied, ignoring his silent pleas. 'We're heading back to our house in Dorset. We moved a year ago. Didn't Ade—'

'It's a lie!' Mama shot to her feet. 'Ade . . . Dorset . . . Will you answer me?'

Ade slid forward in his chair and rested his head on the table. Ife stood up and went to take her bag.

'Where do you think you are going?' Mama snapped, and she sat back down.

'Ade, I am talking to you. Is what she is saying true? Did you leave?'

'Mummy, I—'

'Of course it's true,' Cynthia interjected. 'Ade, let's go.'

'How could you do this to me? All the way to the other side of the country.'

'Mum, it's not that far—'

'A whole year and you didn't even inform me. Are we fighting Adebayo? Or did I carry you inside here for nine months for you to be keeping things like this from me?'

'No, Mum—'

'What would your father say if he was here to see all of this? What would he say, Adebayo?'

'Mum . . . please.' He stared at Cynthia for a few seconds, and she could tell that he was debating something in his mind. When his expression turned from thoughtful to apologetic, Cynthia knew he was about to do something stupid.

'We just wanted it to be a surprise,' he said, rubbing the back of his head.

'Surprise? What do you mean by that?' Mama didn't look at all convinced.

'I mean,' he continued. 'We were planning to invite you to spend next weekend with us, but we didn't have a chance to ask. What with you inviting Ife and all.'

Ife made a 'don't bring me into this' face, but remained silent.

'Next weekend?' Mama's face lit up. 'I will have to check my diary, but—'

'Great,' Ade said, breathing a sigh of relief. 'We're really looking forward to it – right, babe?'

But Cynthia was already storming out of the dining room.

CHAPTER TWO

Ife, present day

'You sure you don't want to go home?' Tayo asks, and Ife nods even though she isn't sure about anything anymore.

They're sitting in Tayo's bright-blue Mini, parked outside the hotel where she and Ade are meant to be spending their wedding night. Her dress is trapped in the door, and Ife wishes Tayo would stop questioning her so she can finally set herself free and tackle the ever-growing to-do list in her head:

1. Cancel their flights.
2. Try to get a partial refund on the honeymoon resort in Saint Lucia.
3. Pretend her life isn't completely falling apart. That her husband hasn't been arrested at their wedding reception and is now being charged with the unthinkable.

After the police carted Ade away, Ife had hoped her guests would take that as their cue to go home, but Mama, who had other ideas, announced that her son was not a criminal, that she was going to collect him from the police station and the celebrations should therefore continue. She'd then grabbed Ade's best friend and lawyer, Robert, and headed down to the police station to 'rescue her son', leaving Ife to fend for herself.

The party had quickly picked up again – Afrobeats blaring from the speakers, a swarm of brightly dressed Nigerians pushing past her as they made their way onto the dance floor.

A few of them approached her, mostly in pairs, eager to have their curiosity satiated. *What happened to your husband? Why was he arrested? Don't tell me he's been doing 419.* The last part was almost always whispered, the guests leaning forward, their eyes sparkling with anticipation as they sipped their Supermalt through a straw, awaiting her answer. *You must stand by your husband, my dear daughter*, they added, their co-conspirator nodding in agreement. *Marriage is for life.*

It was Tayo who had eventually put a stop to the madness, pulling the speakers from their sockets and sending everyone home with their wedding favours in tow.

He is the only one looking out for her, the only one making sure that she's okay. In all the years Tayo has been in her life, Ife has never taken the time to get to know him – a mistake she is now determined to fix.

4. Repay Tayo's kindness.

'Okay,' Tayo says, giving her bare shoulder a gentle squeeze. 'I'll call you in the morning, yeah?'

Ife gives him what she hopes is a reassuring smile before gathering the folds of her dress in her arms and exiting the car. Tayo drives off, leaving her on the cold night road alone.

This she is used to.

The hotel lobby is quiet when Ife enters it through the revolving doors, and she slips off her shoes and walks barefoot over the plush red carpet, her sullied dress flowing behind her as she makes her way towards the front desk. She glances at the large gold-plated clock that sits on the wall behind the clerk. It's already one in the morning, and, despite the day she's had, Ife is relieved that it's so late, that there is no one here to witness her walking through the hotel looking like she belongs in the post-breakup scene of a bad 80s rom-com.

'Ah, Mrs Dolapo.' The clerk, who looks as if he's about to fall off his chair from boredom, sits up, suddenly alert as she approaches his desk. 'We've been expecting you. It *is* Mrs Dolapo, isn't it?' He taps something into his computer, then squints.

Ife confirms her identity. The clerk nods, and there is kindness in his tired eyes.

'Suite 703. I'll send Mr Dolapo straight up when he

gets here.' He winks at her, and Ife smiles weakly as she takes the key.

When she opens the door to their suite, Ife realises too late the mistake she's made in coming here. It lives up to its advertisement as the honeymoon suite, with its floor-to-ceiling windows overlooking the sea and its large empty bed, another unwanted reminder that her husband isn't here to share it with her.

At first, the rose petals look like tiny drops of blood splattered all over the bed, and Ife has to blink several times, squeezing her eyes shut and then opening them again to clear the image from her mind. Two heart-shaped boxes of chocolates sit side by side on the bedside table, along with a bottle of champagne in a melting bucket of ice and two frosted flutes.

She considers leaving, calling Tayo to come and pick her up, but the embarrassment of going back to the clerk to explain the situation or make up a half-baked lie overwhelms her desire to leave.

Instead, she drops her shoes by the door and lies down on the bed, her toes tickling the carpet.

Her phone pings in her Jimmy Choo bridal bag, and with a sigh Ife empties its contents onto the bed. Out fall her powder and a small make-up brush, tear-stained tissues, the bride and groom cake topper she'd swiped when no one was looking, and finally her mobile phone. She enters her passcode, Ade's birthday, to unlock it.

Notification after notification appears on the screen informing her that she's been tagged in this photo and that video. She refuses to click on any of them, afraid that someone has recorded Ade's arrest, that the most earth-shattering moment of her life is about to go viral.

She swipes away each social-media notification with a flick of her thumb, flips over her phone and reaches for the remote to switch on the television. A rerun of *Friends* is on, and Ife grabs a box of chocolates and stuffs two in her mouth at a time. Moments later, half the box is gone and Ife has switched the television off in frustration. A show that had once been a comfort now only reminds her that the drama her life has become will not be resolved in a thirty-minute adventure complete with a laugh track.

She stares at the bottle of champagne, knowing that she can't but desperately wanting to. She grabs the bottle. Looks at the label, contemplating. Slowly she uncorks it, its celebratory pop urging her on. Squeezing her eyes shut, she lifts the cold wet bottle to her lips, and—

Her phone pings again. Ife's eyes fly open. She puts the bottle back on the table and turns her phone back over, hoping for a message from Mama or Ade's lawyer, Robert. Instead, she finds a text from one of her former colleagues who hadn't been able to make it to the wedding.

Girl, wat happened?! Call me!!!

Ife swipes the message away, hurt that her so-called friend

hadn't even bothered to ask how she was doing, that she only seemed interested in hearing the gossip. The fact that Ife has no idea what the gossip is only adds to her frustration.

She swallows back the tears that are threatening to resurface. There's no use feeling sorry for herself – she's spent her entire life doing that. If she wants to know the truth, she'll have to find out for herself.

Robert picks up on the third ring. His voice is hoarse, like he's used up his speaking quota for the day and now he's running on empty.

'How is he?' she asks.

'Hard to say. Better than expected, I think. He's not answering questions very well, which doesn't help. They're insisting on keeping him overnight for more questioning.'

'Can I speak with him?'

'Not tonight. You might be able to see him tomorrow, but considering the ruckus Mama's been making, it's not looking likely.'

Despite everything, Ife smiles. 'That bad, huh?'

'You know how she is.'

'Robert?' Ife swallows the excess saliva that's pooling in her mouth. She wants to ask him the question that's been plaguing her ever since the police slammed the handcuffs on her husband's wrists and dragged him away. But deep down, buried in the part of her mind she's been avoiding since the night Ade proposed to her, she already knows the answer.

This is about Cynthia.

There's a moment of hesitation before he responds, and she can tell he knows what she's about to ask.

'Get some rest, Fey,' he says gently. 'He's going to need you at your best.'

With that, the line goes dead, and Ife stares at her phone, debating whether or not she should call him back. She is Ade's wife now after all, and she deserves to know the truth.

Except, if this is about Cynthia Bennet, she isn't sure she wants to know.

Just as she's about to dial Robert's number, Ife's phone pings again. This time it's a text message from an unknown number.

youll pay for what you did.

CHAPTER THREE

Eleven weeks before Cynthia's disappearance

'You're up early.'

Cynthia turned her attention from the suitcase she was packing to find Ade bare-chested in the doorway of their bedroom, his arms wrapped around his blanket and pillow, his expression half-questioning, half-horrified as his eyes darted from her face to her suitcase and back to her face again.

Cynthia ignored him and shoved her conditioner in with the rest of her hair products. She'd hoped to be dressed and out of the house by the time Ade woke up, but instead she was fresh from her shower, tiny droplets rolling down her forehead as she braced herself for a conversation she would have given her right foot to avoid.

'I thought your hip-hop class wasn't until this afternoon.'

Ade was standing behind her now, his breath, warm and heavy, tickling the back of her neck. Cynthia understood the unspoken question in his statement, knew he wanted her to explain why his girlfriend was packing a suitcase at seven o'clock on a Thursday morning when they didn't have a holiday planned.

'Please just talk to me,' Ade whispered when she didn't respond. His arms were wrapped around her, his lips pressed against her ear. 'I'm sorry, okay?'

Part of her wanted to melt into him, to enclose herself in his arms and pretend that awful dinner had never happened. She was tired of fighting, tired of being angry, but whenever she remembered what Mama had said and how Ade hadn't uttered a single word in her defence, she couldn't bring herself to look at him.

Sure, maybe he was sorry, but since Mama was still planning to make an appearance in a few days' time, it was clear to Cynthia that nothing had changed. Not really.

So, instead, she pulled her towel tight and moved past him towards the wardrobe, using their bed as a barrier between them. She could feel him watching her as she pulled out a handful of t-shirts, none of which she was even planning to take with her, and added them to the ever-growing pile on the bed. A breeze came in from the open window, and she shivered.

'Here.' He picked up her favourite jumper from the pile of clothes and offered it to her – a white flag Cynthia had no intention of acknowledging.

'Why you being like this?' he asked. 'I'm the one who woke up at stupid o'clock in the morning to find you . . .' He swallowed. 'To find you're leaving me. And now you're giving me the silent treatment.'

'It's just for a couple of days.'

'Those are a lot of clothes for a couple of days.'

Cynthia shrugged. 'I like to keep my options open.'

'Meaning?'

Cynthia returned to packing her suitcase.

'So you want me to just cut her off? My own mother?'

Cynthia narrowed her eyes at him. 'Are you mad? You're the one who's been lying to her all this time. Who sat there in silence while she insulted me to my face, and then, to top it all off, you invite her here, to our home, without even talking to me first. And now all you have to say for yourself is *Sorry babe, I didn't mean it.*'

'She's my *mother*, Cynthia. What do you want me to do?'

Cynthia slammed her now-too-full suitcase shut and tried but failed to zip it up. They'd already argued about this a dozen and one times, and Ade had already insisted he couldn't uninvite Mama, so the answer to his ridiculous question was . . .

'Nothing,' Cynthia snapped. '*That's.*' Push. '*Why.*' Push. '*I'm.*' Push. '*Leaving.*' She flung her suitcase open again and started throwing out the clothes she'd just packed, piling them onto the floor behind her.

'You know she didn't mean what she said, right?'

'Sure,' Cynthia said. 'She didn't *mean* to try and marry you off to *Fey-Fey*. It was all just one big misunderstanding.'

'Ah, so that's what this is about.' Ade folded his arms.

'Even though it was you who said you weren't ready to get married.'

'You know what? Fuck you, Ade.' It was a line she rarely crossed, and Ade looked like she'd just kicked him in the balls. Cynthia turned to pick up a pair of jeans, trying to decide whether they would look better on her or on Ade's head.

'Will you stop packing for one second and just listen to me?'

Ade was moving towards her again, a determined look in his eye, and Cynthia took several steps back, nearing the open window which overlooked the chapel that gave the village its name. Its bell clanged in the distance, signalling the start of the hour.

He looked down at her and lifted a strand of her ever-shrinking hair from her face.

'Don't you have to do your little twist thingies before your hair goes all . . .' He made a balloon with his mouth and then smiled his stupid, irresistible smile. Her anger, a shield against his charm, began to dissolve, leaving her feeling helpless.

'You promised you wouldn't let her come between us,' she said with a sigh, rubbing at the tightness in her chest. She was *not* going to cry.

'And she won't.' He leant past her to shut the open window. 'If you stay, she won't.'

'I can't. Not after what she said.'

'But I love you,' he insisted.

Cynthia shook her head. His words were too flimsy to withstand the weight of what he'd done.

'Love isn't a weapon, Ade. You can't use it to win a fight.'

He seemed to mull this over, as if the idea hadn't occurred to him before.

'Okay,' he said, sounding defeated. 'So, what now?'

'The apartment above the studio,' she replied, trying not to let her disappointment show. She'd wanted him to fight for them, to put her first. But once again he was giving up. 'Janine said I can use it whenever I need to.'

'And it's just for a few days? Until Mum leaves?'

Cynthia nodded.

'Come here,' he said, dragging her into a hug. He held her tightly, resting his chin on her head. 'I'm just trying to protect us,' he whispered. 'Like I promised.'

Then why did it feel like he was letting her go?

At the studio, only five of the ten students who'd registered turned up for her class, and although Cynthia knew she should be grateful that anyone had come at all, she was fed up with everything going wrong.

When they'd moved here, she'd been worried that no one would be interested in taking her classes, and so far she'd mostly been right. Windchapel's main attractions were a tea room that only opened at the weekend and a seven-hundred-year-old chapel with beautiful acoustics that drew people to the lonely hill it sat on.

Although Cynthia loved how peaceful it was here, she knew deep down that despite Ade's optimism, it would take divine intervention to make this studio in this location a success. She wasn't in any position to be asking God for favours, but she'd promised Ade she'd at least try and make it work. So, when she'd received a random email letting her know that the recently renovated space was available to rent long-term, she'd jumped at the chance.

Apparently, her frustrated posts to her two thousand Instagram followers had caught someone's attention.

When she'd officially opened two months earlier, there had been an initial burst of interest, mostly housewives looking for something to break up the monotony of their daily chores. But by week three, her numbers had dwindled so much that she'd had to cancel half her classes indefinitely. Maybe it was her teaching and not her location that was putting people off.

She glanced at her students. They weren't professionals by any stretch of the imagination, but they were managing to put the steps she'd taught them together just fine, and from the looks on their faces, they seemed to be enjoying themselves. Then what? Maybe she needed to be friendlier, interact with them a little more.

'Okay guys. Good job,' she said when the class ended, but they all dashed out of the door before Cynthia had a chance to say anything else.

With a sigh, she turned back towards the mirror, sat down on the floor and began to stretch. Usually, the dance floor was the one place she could let go of all her worries, the place where she could be her truest self, and, for the most part, that hadn't changed. But the stress of trying to turn her passion into a business was starting to take its toll.

After a few moments of stretching, she stood up again and hit play on the remote control. Emeli Sandé filled the room, and Cynthia glided to the floor, rolled herself into a small ball and began to unravel herself, allowing the music to take her again.

'Knock knock.' A man's voice interrupted Cynthia mid-pirouette, and she stumbled over her feet, her ankle twisting awkwardly as she landed on the hardwood floor with a thud. She grabbed her foot, squeezing her eyes shut in an attempt to push the pain away.

'Shit, I'm sorry, I didn't mean to scare you.' The concerned voice was right behind her now, and Cynthia tried her best not to groan in embarrassment. Although she'd tripped and fallen many times in her nearly decade-long career, she didn't want her students to think she was incompetent.

'Hey, are you all right?' the voice said, and Cynthia felt a comforting hand on her shoulder. 'Should I get some help or something?'

Cynthia lifted her head, and in the mirror a tall man with curly dark-brown hair, a little too long for him, was staring back at her, his striking green eyes observing her with concern.

'I'm fine,' she replied, waving him away. 'I just tripped a little.' She wrestled to her feet, a little too quickly, apparently, because she nearly fell again. Except this time the stranger with the green eyes and sparkling smile caught her in his arms.

'Steady now,' he said, holding her up. If her skin had been fairer, she would have blushed red. The man glanced down at her foot and made a hissing sound.

'Looks broken,' he said.

Cynthia rolled her eyes, trying to recover from her earlier embarrassment.

'Remind me again where you got your medical degree?'

'Oxford, actually . . .'

'Oh.' Cynthia looked up from her ankle and into his grinning face.

'Nah, I'm kidding,' he said. 'But I did get you to smile. Here,' he added, pointing to a couple of stools on the other side of the studio. 'You should probably sit down.'

'Thanks,' Cynthia said as she settled onto one of them.

She rolled her ankle even though it was painful. 'You can go if you want. I'll probably have to cancel the class anyway.'

'What makes you think I'm here for the class?' he asked, sitting on the floor next to her. He was dressed in a hoodie with a flock of multicoloured goats imprinted on the front. Its sleeves were rolled up to reveal hairless arms, a dreamcatcher tattooed on the right and a collection of beaded bracelets in various shades of black and brown on the left. Not exactly jazz-class attire.

She made a 'what are you doing here, then?' face, not wanting to say the words out loud in case they sounded as rude as they did in her head.

'Oh, right,' he said, as if he'd forgotten he hadn't introduced himself. 'I'm Mark. I'm moving into the apartment upstairs.' His extended hand fell away when Cynthia didn't take it, and his smile crumpled into a frown. 'I haven't gone to the wrong place, have I? You're Cynthia, right? Cynthia Bennet?'

Cynthia nodded.

'Oh, thank God.' He clutched his chest and breathed a sigh of relief. His Mancunian accent was more prominent now, and Cynthia smiled at the sense of familiarity it created. 'I'm not meant to be moving in until tomorrow, but I thought I'd pop in and say hi. Janine said it would be all right?'

Cynthia vaguely remembered Janine, the building manager, emailing her about someone moving into the apartment above the studio, but she hadn't realised it would be so soon. There went her Mama escape plan.

'Sorry, I completely forgot. Nice to meet you.'

'You, too,' he said. 'Shame about the circumstances though.' He looked down at her foot, and Cynthia followed the direction of his eyes. 'Sorry for interrupting you. You looked like you were in pretty good form there, but I felt a bit stalkerish just standing there watching you. How's it feeling?'

Cynthia flexed her foot forward and then back again, the way she'd been taught.

'Better,' she said. 'It's probably just a mild sprain.'

'Want me to take a look?'

'I thought you weren't a doctor?'

'I'm not.' He shrugged. 'But my wife tells me I'm pretty good at foot rubs.' He shook his head as if he'd just remembered something. 'Sorry, *ex*-wife. Soon, anyway. I've got to get used to saying that. Here, let me see.'

And perhaps because she was in pain, or because she was still angry with Ade, or maybe because it had been ages since anyone had been this nice to her, Cynthia slipped off her trainer and placed her foot into Mark's waiting hands.

CHAPTER FOUR

Ife, present day

This is your home, this is your home, this is your home.

Ife dips her hand into the pocket of her hoodie and pulls out the key to the cottage Cynthia and Ade had once shared. She'd spent months mentally preparing for this moment, her discomfort eased by the knowledge that Ade would be right by her side when she moved in.

Except now she is alone, still in her wedding dress because she couldn't bear to ask one of the hotel staff to help her out of it.

She'd spent most of the day hiding in the hotel suite, debating whether or not she should go to the police station or come here, wishing that she'd kept her flat for a few more weeks so she had somewhere else to go, anywhere but this seemingly innocuous place she's now meant to call her own.

From the outside, it certainly looks like a home, the kind you might find on the front of a Christmas card. A layer of frost covers the brick-layered exterior and the grass out front. A warm overhead lamp lights up when she moves, urging her to come in.

But Ife isn't fooled by the cosy aesthetic, and she glances around the empty street, half expecting a neighbour to jump out and accuse her of breaking in.

Forcing the thought from her mind, she pushes the door open, tugging her suitcase behind her.

The house is dark and somehow colder than outside. Ife scans the hallway for the boxes Ade had brought from her flat the day before the wedding. They are nowhere to be found, and Ife wonders if he's moved them, if the police have realised their mistake and sent him home.

'Ade?' she calls out, gently shutting the door. The sound reverberates through the house and yet Ife can't shake the feeling that she isn't alone. Surely Ade would have called her if he'd been released.

She calls his name again and winds her way to the living room, unsure of whether to hope for a response or silence.

She doesn't want to be in this house alone, but she also isn't ready to . . .

Ife freezes.

CHAPTER FIVE

Eleven weeks before Cynthia's disappearance

'Wait, so you're a *record* producer?'

Cynthia was still in her studio with Mark, her sprained ankle and fight with Ade pushed to the back of her mind.

'Yeah,' he said, rubbing his eyebrow with the edge of his index finger.

'Worked with anyone famous?'

In another life, Cynthia had wanted to be a singer, had even led the choir at her father's church, until he kicked her out of the congregation and her childhood home. She hadn't spoken to her parents or sung in public since.

It wasn't until recently, with Ade's encouragement, that she'd started to rediscover her passion for singing, posting the occasional cover on her Instagram stories, grateful that they disappeared after twenty-four hours. To hear that Mark was a record producer felt like a sign, although of what Cynthia wasn't sure yet.

'Maybe.' Mark's eyes twinkled in response to her question.

'Being coy now, are we?'

'I prefer humble,' Mark said.

'Fine, fine,' Cynthia waved him away. Her smart watch vibrated on her wrist reminding her that her next class was due to begin, and she was yet to cancel it. Not that it mattered anyway since no one had bothered to turn up.

Cynthia tried to tell herself that this was just business, that it was nothing personal, but it still stung. She didn't want to give up, but sometimes it felt like the odds were stacked so highly against her that she didn't have a choice. Like moving to Windchapel really had been a mistake.

'Everything all right?'

Cynthia nodded, feeling the last of her resolve crumble.

'This is all just . . .' – she swallowed, motioning around the room with her hand – 'a lot harder than I thought it would be.' She couldn't believe she was crying in front of a stranger, and she apologised, wiping her eye with the palm of her hand.

'Hey.' Mark leant forward to give her shoulder a squeeze. 'You opened this studio, what, two months ago?'

Cynthia nodded, glad that at least someone other than her five students had heard about her classes. 'I'm just . . . not sure if I'm cut out for this.'

'Course you are,' Mark insisted. 'You seem smart. Brave. Definitely talented. Whatever's going on, I'm sure you'll figure it out.'

'You got all that from one conversation?'

Mark shrugged. 'Occupational hazard.' There was that grin again. She was such a sucker for gorgeous smiles.

'Thanks.' Cynthia sniffed and managed a weak smile in return.

'Actually, I've got to go,' she told him.

Now that Mark was staying in the flat above the studio, she had no choice but to go home and start the Mama argument all over again. She couldn't tell Mark to find somewhere else to live, and Ade would never let it go if she moved in with another man. As hurt as she was, she wasn't ready to give up on their relationship yet. Which meant she was back to square one – trying to find a way to deal with Ade's mother.

'Can I drop you somewhere?'

'Nah, I think I should be fine to drive.'

Cynthia stood. Pain radiated through her ankle, and she sat back down again. 'Or not.'

They hobbled out of the studio, Mark holding Cynthia's bags, Cynthia holding on to Mark, both of them staring down at Cynthia's foot as they moved. When they turned the corner, they slammed straight into Ade, all three of them stumbling back from the impact.

'Are you okay?' Ade asked, leaning forward to stabilise her even though Mark was already holding her.

'I'm fine.' Cynthia brushed him off. 'What are you doing here, anyway?'

'I brought you lunch,' Ade said, lifting a takeaway bag. 'But it looks like you already have company.'

'I'm Mark,' Mark said. 'Not a doctor, by the way.' He offered Ade his hand, and Ade shook it. 'I'm moving into the apartment upstairs.'

'Sorry?' Ade asked, immediately dropping Mark's hand.

'The apartment upstairs,' Mark repeated. 'I'm moving in.'

Ade turned to Cynthia, his eyes wide and questioning.

'What?' She was getting a headache just imagining where this conversation was going.

'You didn't tell me—'

'Because I didn't *know*, Ade. Jesus Christ.'

'Okay, so you're coming home, yeah?' He was staring at Mark, who'd taken a sudden interest in his shoelaces. Cynthia let Ade's question hang in the air, and smiled to herself as his jaw began to tick the way it always did when he was getting annoyed.

'Hello?' he snapped.

Cynthia shrugged, knowing it would piss him off even more. 'This is my home now,' she said, wistfully looking around as if she was seeing the place for the first time. 'I can stay in one of the other rooms. I'm sure Mark won't mind.'

Mark shuffled next to her, but, to his credit, he didn't say a thing.

Ade muttered something that sounded a lot like *the hell you will*, but Cynthia didn't have a chance to confirm because the next thing she knew she was being lifted off the ground and over Ade's shoulder.

'Are you mad? Put me down.'

Ade ignored her and snapped his fingers at Mark.

'Oya, bags,' he said, extending the hand that held the takeaway bags. Mark silently handed them over, and Ade stormed out of the studio, deposited Cynthia into his car and drove off in the opposite direction of their once peaceful cottage.

CHAPTER SIX

Ife, present day

Ife's eyes dart around the living room as she struggles to take in the unexpected chaos.

She. Is. Everywhere.

She had just started to make peace with the fact that she would be living in Cynthia's old house, that she might stumble across a few of Cynthia's things when she moved in – a lost earring or a misplaced comb.

But this . . .

She starts with the floor.

Photographs of Ade and Cynthia are laid out like a relationship walk of fame, each picture an untimely reminder of their once perfect lives together.

There's one of Ade and Cynthia eating ice cream, of Ade and Cynthia on a boat, of Ade and Cynthia at a club, at a wedding, at a concert. Ade and Cynthia huddled together at the local beach. Ade and Cynthia, Ade and Cynthia, Ade and Cynthia.

Ife gathers the photographs, following the path down someone else's memory lane. She stares at the photo on the beach, at Ade's arms wrapped around Cynthia's waist as he kisses her on the cheek. Cynthia is gazing right at her, and Ife's chest tightens.

It's just a photo, she tells herself, dropping the pictures face down on the sofa where there are piles of women's clothes that don't belong to her. T-shirts, leggings, bras and that unmistakable smell of Cantu leave-in conditioner entwined in the fabric of the air.

Ife presses her hand over her mouth, afraid that she might scream or throw up. Gripping the side of the sofa, she squeezes her eyes shut, tries to keep the room from spinning by taking a deep breath.

And another.

And another.

When she opens her eyes, Ade is standing in the doorway.

Still in his wedding tux, rumpled shirt unbuttoned, tie hanging from his shoulder, he looks just as dishevelled as she feels. His uncombed hair has sprung greys overnight, and his big toe peeks from his left sock, showing off the pre-wedding pedicure she'd taken him to get.

'You're home,' she says, though it's more of a question than a statement, and it isn't the question she really wants to ask.

'Robert just dropped me off.' He makes his way towards the sofa, zeroing in on the overturned photos.

'Those bastards.' He rifles through them, pauses to focus

on one of them, before dropping them all back on the chair. 'I don't know why they would do this,' he tells her. 'But I promise I'll sort this out. I'll get your boxes from outside, and we can unpack together, just like we planned.'

Ife follows Ade's gaze to the back garden, and, sure enough, her boxes are there, their contents strewn across the frost-covered grass.

Despite Ade's suspicions and her limited knowledge of police procedure, Ife is almost certain this isn't the handiwork of detectives rummaging for clues. There are no drawers hastily thrown open, no overturned lamps, and every cushion is still in its place.

There's only one person who would have been angry enough to do this and it isn't her, or Ade, or the police.

She shivers and turns her attention back to Ade, willing him to look at her.

When he finally does, he observes her with bloodshot eyes, his expression unreadable.

'What happened with the police?' she asks, unsure of what else to say.

Ade releases an exhausted breath.

'Cynthia,' he says. 'She's been missing for months, apparently.' His voice cracks as he says this, and he collapses onto the pile on the sofa.

Ife sits next to him, her hands, suddenly stiff, clasped in her lap.

Silence stretches like a rubber band between them, neither of them wanting to let go first. It reminds her of that day, just before her sixteenth birthday, when she'd planned to tell him that she kind of, sort of, liked him as more than friend.

He'd been away at boarding school for several months, and they'd chatted almost every day on MSN, playing RuneScape and reminiscing about the good old days. Sometimes, it seemed like he was flirting with her or at the very least that he wished that she was there, and Ife often found herself lying in bed on her laptop waiting for him to come online, her heart doing a little jump when his name popped up on her screen.

A few days earlier, he'd told her that he was coming home for the Easter holidays, and they'd planned to meet up. Her best friend Demi had given her a makeover for the occasion, swapping her usual uniform of Afro puffs and a baggy t-shirt for straight hair and a boob tube.

On the day of their meet-up he'd shown up at the dessert place on Old Kent Road late, arm in arm with his new girlfriend, Chantelle, who was dressed in a baggy t-shirt and whom he hadn't even bothered to tell her about.

Ife had sat there in shamed silence, and he'd just stared at her, waiting for her to say something, his right eyebrow slightly raised as if he was challenging her, although to what Ife wasn't sure.

Now, Ade slips his arm around her and pulls her close, holding her like she's his lifeline. The smell of his aftershave has managed to stay with him, the warm, musky scent just about masking his body odour.

'They're trying to pin this on me with some angry ex bullshit,' Ade says when she still doesn't respond. He leans his head against her shoulder. 'I told them the breakup was mutual. That me and Cynthia were still friends, but . . .'

Ife shifts in her seat. That wasn't what he'd told her when he'd proposed three months earlier.

'They only let me go because they don't have enough evidence for a murder charge, just a statement from a so-called witness. No corpse, no case, as Robert so charmingly put it.'

Ife shakes her head. 'But why now?' she asks him, before she can stop herself.

'Sorry?'

'It's just . . .' Ife plays with the zip on her hoodie. 'A bit strange, right? If she's been missing all this time, why are the police questioning you now?'

Ade withdraws his arm from around her. 'How the fuck should I know?'

His eyes meet hers. Ife knows Ade too well, and she knows Ade knows this too, because he sighs.

'Fine,' he says, looking away. 'They did question me a few months back after someone reported her missing. I didn't think anything of it . . . I figured she'd just gone back to London or Manchester after we broke up.' He glances at Ife. 'Don't look at me like that.'

'Like what?'

'Like you're rewriting our entire history with me as the villain.'

'I'm not,' she says. 'I just wish you'd told me. Maybe I could have helped.'

Ade releases a pained breath. 'I can't believe she's gone,' he whispers. 'I know she wasn't perfect but . . . shit.'

Tears make a trail down Ade's face. Ife hesitates before taking his hand and uses one of his fingers to catch one. He sniffs and gives her a sad smile.

'She could still be alive,' she tells him. 'At the very least, it would explain this mess, and my stuff outside.'

Ade doesn't respond. Instead, he wraps his arm around her again. His body is aflame, and Ife presses the back of her hand against his forehead.

'You're getting sick,' she tells him, and he leans his forehead against hers and closes his eyes.

'Good thing I have you to take care of me, then,' he whispers.

Before Ife can respond, a loud bang, like a door slamming shut, stops her. Ade jumps away from her like they'd been caught doing something inappropriate.

'Ade—'

'Don't. Move.' His terror-filled eyes dart around the room.

Ife frowns. 'Maybe you left the back door open?'

She gets up to check, but Ade grips her hand so tightly, her knuckles crack.

'Don't go,' he says.

'Let me just—'

'Please,' he says. 'Please.'

Ife studies his panicked face, confused by his reaction.

'Okay,' she whispers. 'Okay.'

He pulls her into him, closing his eyes as he holds her close. His breathing slows, and, after a few moments, he plants a gentle kiss on her cheek.

'You looked beautiful yesterday,' he says, his warm breath tickling her ear. His lips move from her cheek to her neck, as if moments earlier they hadn't been discussing his missing, possibly dead ex-girlfriend. Ife rolls her shoulders back to shake him off, torn between shifting away from him and pulling him closer, between comforting him and wanting to escape, to anywhere but here.

'We can't,' she tells him. 'Not now.'

'Fey.' He lifts her chin so she's forced to look into his eyes. They hold each other's gaze, and, yes, she sees desire there, but also something else, something Ife can't quite identify.

'Fey,' he says again, his eyes welling up, and Ife softens. How can she reject him now? The man she's fought so desperately to have?

'Okay,' she says, and he slowly reaches for her hoodie, unzipping it to reveal the bust of her wedding dress.

He sighs, tracing her collarbone with his lips. His kiss is impatient, desperate, like he's being chased and she is his only refuge. Ife can't tell if he's desperate for her or to not be alone. She knows she shouldn't care, that it should only matter that he is here, now, that he wants to be with her.

And yet the thought stays with her when he kisses her again, is still there when he finally releases her from her wedding dress and pulls her underwear over her hips, the silky material landing on the floor next to them.

It's only when he pushes Cynthia's belongings from the couch and covers her body with his that her worries begin to fade. She's reminded that he chose *her*, he married *her*, and, although she hasn't told him yet, he is the father of *her* child. He wouldn't be here if he didn't love her.

But then he says her name:

Cynthia.

Cynthia.

Cynthia.

The word echoing like a siren in her head.

Ife struggles to get away from him, scrambling for her clothes and her phone before locking herself in the cupboard next to the living room. She flicks the light switch and is greeted by a room filled with more of Cynthia's belongings. Ife snaps the light back off, her energy evaporating as she slouches against the door.

Ade is pounding on it, begging her to let him in. But she isn't ready to face him. Part of her feels like she only has herself to blame. She should have listened to her instincts when they told her they were getting married too soon. But this was Ade. How could she *not* marry him?

Her phone buzzes on the floor next to her, and she reaches for it. Anything to drown out Ade and her thoughts.

A link from an unknown number with the headline: BODY FOUND IN SEARCH FOR MISSING DANCER illuminates the screen.

Before she has a chance to click the article, her phone vibrates again.

pack your bags or i will tell him everything

CHAPTER SEVEN

Eleven weeks before Cynthia's disappearance

'Where are you taking me?'

Ade didn't respond, but a few moments later they were pulling up to the harbour where Cynthia's boat was docked.

While the short drive seemed to have calmed Ade down, Cynthia was now boiling with rage. That morning, she'd been willing to *maybe* give him another chance, but now it felt like the only way forward was out.

Ade got out of the car in silence and shimmied around the front to open the door for her.

'You coming?' he asked, dangling her boat key, the Afro girl figurine Tayo had given her for her birthday swinging from the chain.

'Do you even know how to sail?'

'I was in the yacht club at Oxford.'

'Of course you were,' Cynthia muttered.

'Sorry?'

'Nothing. Help me up, please.'

Ade pulled her from her seat, and Cynthia limped away from him.

It was still unseasonably warm, and a gentle breeze blew in from the waterfront. Cynthia took a deep breath, savouring the salty sea air. It was a smart move on Ade's part, to bring her somewhere he knew would calm her down.

'What happened to your leg?' he asked when he noticed her limping.

'Minor accident.'

'Need me to carry you?'

Cynthia glared at him, and he held his hands up in surrender, a cheeky grin tugging at the corner of his mouth.

Soon the polished white exterior and light-blue stripes of her beloved boat were in view. Cynthia had fallen in love the moment she'd seen it glistening in the sunlight one May afternoon a few months after they'd arrived in Windchapel.

She'd struck up a conversation with the elderly owner who'd told her he was moving abroad and was looking to sell. She'd been surprised to find that she didn't need a licence to sail the boat, only insanely high insurance coverage. But she couldn't put a price on the sense of peace this beautiful little vessel gave her.

Now, as she waved at the dockmaster on duty, his long blond hair flapping in the wind as he wiped his glasses with his t-shirt, she was reminded that Windchapel wasn't *all* bad.

'Who's that?' Ade asked her, holding his hand out to help her onto the boat.

'Don't start.'

'I was just asking.'

'If we're going to argue then I'd rather do it on dry land.'

He turned away from her and fumbled with the key to start the boat. After a few tries, it rumbled to life, and they were off.

For a while, the only sound was the engine humming behind them and the boat slashing through the water. From the distance, Cynthia could see the top of the hill that gave the town its name. She and Ade often took the well-trodden path to the foot of the hill and climbed to the top to enjoy a picnic, dangling their feet over the edge of the cliff as they ate. She wished she could go back there, back to a time when it was just the two of them, embarking on a new adventure.

'I get why you like coming out here,' Ade said softly, turning around to face her once they were on the open water, away from the other vessels. 'It's calming. Meditative.'

He sat down, leaning his knee against hers. 'I've been thinking about what you said this morning. About me choosing my mother over you.'

'So, you agree?'

He shook his head. 'Handling my mother is like navigating a minefield, Cynthia. One wrong move and everything gets destroyed. I thought on some basic level you knew that.'

'I'm not psychic, Ade. If I was, I wouldn't have listened when you *promised* me this wouldn't happen.'

She expected him to defend himself the way he always did, but instead he sighed.

'I know,' he said. 'It's just . . . usually better to let her have her way.'

'So you're never going to stand up to her? Not even for us?'

'I'm *trying*, Cynthia . . .'

Cynthia looked away from him. It was hard for her to believe that a man who ran a successful tech company, commanding the respect of dozens of employees, couldn't defend against his own mother. She said this to him, and his expression grew sad.

'I guess it's different with her. It has to be.'

'Because—?'

It was Ade's turn to shift away. Cynthia knew he struggled to explain why his mother had such a hold on him, but this time she wasn't going to let it go without an answer. Not when their relationship was falling apart.

'Because—?' she repeated.

'Because she protected me when I didn't deserve it.'

Cynthia wanted to point out that that was her motherly duty, but what did she know? Her own mother had just sat there in silence when her father booted her out of their house, and she hadn't spoken to either of them since, despite her sister Valerie's sporadic messages urging her to call them.

Besides, Ade seemed to be talking about something more complicated than that. She began to ask him, but he stopped her.

'I know it doesn't make sense,' he said. 'So let me be clear. I love you. I love being with you, I love waking up next to you, I love having you in my life. Everything I do, especially when it comes to my mother, is to keep things that way. When have I ever *not* done everything in my power to look after you?'

It was true. From the moment he'd spotted her standing in the snow outside a corner shop by Peckham Library with a dead phone and no way to get to her performance, he'd been protective of her.

He'd offered her a lift, and after she'd searched his car to make sure he wasn't a killer, he'd driven her to the venue, asking her about the show she was in and telling her about his short-lived career as an architect and his shift to entrepreneurship.

They'd arrived an hour later, only to discover that her show had been cancelled. As consolation, he'd taken her to a fancy French bistro where he'd gently teased her for posting photos of her food on Instagram.

The next morning, she'd woken up in hospital. She'd had an allergic reaction after unknowingly swiping a cheese-ball-shaped shrimp puff from his plate, and was surprised to find that Ade hadn't left her side.

'This is definitely one for the Gram,' she'd said, smiling up at him, for once not caring that she probably looked as awful as she felt. He'd stayed. No man had ever done that before.

'I'm just glad you're okay,' he replied, his eyes struggling to stay open. 'I wouldn't have been able to live with myself otherwise.'

But that was then, and none of that mattered now. Not if protecting her meant letting his mother run their lives.

'So I take it that means she's still coming this weekend then?' As usual, he was all talk and no action.

Ade shook his head. 'I called her earlier. I couldn't cancel . . . all hell would break loose if I did. But I told her we needed to reschedule. It's up to you when she comes,' he said.

It was a start. Not exactly what she wanted but better than she'd hoped. She just wished he'd thought of this earlier, before the damage was done.

'Okay,' she said. She stroked the space behind his ear, and he turned to face her again. 'On one condition.'

'Anything.'

'You let Tayo come too.'

Ade shook his head. 'Trust me, he has better things to do.'

'What is it with you two? He gets it from your mother as well, you know. You lot need to stick together.'

'Fine.' He sighed. 'If Tayo *wants* to come, he can. But believe me, babe, you're asking for trouble.'

But she didn't believe him. In fact, for the first time since the night of the dinner, Cynthia felt a sense of hope, and she leant in to kiss him. His lips were cold and salty, and he let out a long breath, releasing the tension between them.

'Since we're on the topic of making amends,' he said, leaning back but keeping her hand in his. 'There's something else I need to talk to you about.'

'I'm listening.'

'It's about Ife.'

He paused, and Cynthia shrugged, ignoring the prickling feeling on the back of her neck. 'I have nothing against her,' she said. 'Can't have a problem with someone I don't know.'

'Good,' Ade said, grazing his thumb over her knuckles. 'Because I offered her a job. She starts on Monday.'

CHAPTER EIGHT

Ife, present day

The pebbles are digging into Ife's bare feet, but she doesn't move, barely even blinks as she stares out at the foggy waters where Cynthia's body was found.

After spending the night hiding in the cupboard, ignoring Ade's pleas for forgiveness, she'd slipped out into the cold winter morning and found herself here, holding a bouquet of flowers she can't quite bring herself to lay. Although she knows in her heart of hearts that he is innocent, that neither of them is to blame, the facts remain the same:

Cynthia was murdered.

Her husband is a suspect.

Someone is threatening to destroy their marriage.

And so she does the only thing she can do and kneels to place the flowers she bought next to a bouquet of lilies and a damp teddy bear, resting against the bins that hold each end of the police cordon.

I miss you C, the card reads, a sketch of a boat scribbled next to it. Ife wonders if she should have written a note too, then realises that Cynthia would not have wanted her platitudes, even if she was still alive to read them.

'Are you okay?' A voice next to her interrupts her thoughts. She turns to find a man without a jacket has materialised next to her, his curly brown hair tousled by the wind. He offers her a tissue, and she takes it, dabbing at the tears in her eyes as she rises to her feet.

'She used to love taking her boat out here,' he says, staring out at the sea. His naked arms are covered in goosebumps, and yet Ife spots a wet patch on his t-shirt: sweat. 'Whenever she was sad or lonely,' the man continues. 'She'd drive down here and take her boat out. Said it made her feel alive.' His voice breaks, and he squeezes his t-shirt like he's trying to wring his pain away. When he turns his gaze back to Ife, the look in his sore red eyes makes her feel like he can see right through her.

'This can't be easy for you either,' he adds.

Ife steps away from him, reminding herself that this man could be anyone. It was foolish of her to come here alone, knowing that someone is watching her, that there is a killer on the loose.

He seems to notice her discomfort and apologises, explains that he doesn't mean any harm.

'Your picture was in the paper, and when I saw you over here, I thought you might want to talk.' He pulls the folded page from his pocket and hands it to her. The photo shows Ade being handcuffed, Ife standing behind him. It is like being right there, reliving that moment all over again. Panic rises in Ife's chest, and she suddenly finds it difficult to breathe, like she too is drowning.

'Here, sit down,' the man urges, and Ife obeys, ignoring the pebbles poking through her joggers. They sit in silence for a few moments, Ife fiddling with her wedding ring while she waits for the world to stop spinning. She can feel the man watching her intently, and she forces herself to speak.

'Did you know her well, then?' she asks.

He nods. 'We lived together for a bit, before she disappeared.'

'So you two were . . . ?'

He sighs. 'It was complicated. Her ex, your husband, was still hanging around, which didn't help.'

'You think he did this, don't you?' Ife asks, the panic threatening to resurface. 'That's why you wanted to talk to me.'

A wave crashes against the shore, lapping at the pebbles before returning home.

'I think his arrest speaks for itself,' he finally says. 'But it doesn't matter what I think,' he adds. 'What do you believe?'

'I know he loved her.' As much as it hurts to admit, it is a truth she can't deny. 'Ade would never hurt someone he loves.'

'Even if that someone rejected his marriage proposal?'

Ife shakes her head. 'That's not true.' Ade had ended it

with Cynthia, not the other way round, so either this man has no idea what he's talking about, or . . .

Ife stands to her feet. Either way, she is done.

She expects the man to stand too, but instead he removes the necklace he's wearing and dangles it in front of her, its intricate design reminding her of something far closer to home.

'Can . . . can I see that?'

He hands it to her, and Ife's breath catches in her throat.

It is almost an exact replica of the engagement ring she's just been fiddling with, except the gemstones are a blueish grey instead of emerald – the same shade of grey as the winter sea, which has now suddenly quietened.

'Tasteless bastard,' the man mutters, eyeing Ife's ring.

Ife jumps to Ade's defence, and then stops herself. He's right, it is tasteless.

'Doesn't make him a murderer though, does it?'

'It makes him a very strong suspect.'

'I could say the same thing about you.'

The man sighs and rises to his feet. 'I'm only trying to help,' he tells her, and there is something in the way he says this that makes it seem like he's the kind of person who's always *just trying to help*, sticking his nose in where it doesn't belong.

'Yeah, well, I don't want your help,' she tells him, holding out the necklace with the ring.

'Keep it,' he says, digging his hands into his pockets. 'And if there's even a tiny part of you that questions what happened, that deep down knows the truth, just call me, okay? My number's on the back of the paper I gave you.'

Before Ife has a chance to protest, he is gone, just as swiftly and as quietly as he first appeared.

She holds the ring in her palm. What is he expecting her to do with it?

She slips her own ring off her finger and replaces it with the one Ade had given to Cynthia. It seems more beautiful than hers somehow. She takes it off again and looks at both rings side by side in her hand, wondering what to do next.

If she gives Cynthia's ring back to Ade, he'll probably ask her where she got it from, and how could she possibly explain that? *A strange man who thinks you murdered your ex gave it to me.* She could hold on to it, hide it until the time was right to bring it up. Or maybe she could keep it for him. When all of this was finally over, she could give it to him as a gift, to let him know that she understood.

Ife shakes her head at how ridiculous her thoughts are. She needs to stop doing this, needs to stop pretending like she can fix everything. She can't.

Cynthia's ring, she realises, is not her problem. She doesn't owe her anything she doesn't owe Ade anything either for that matter. Besides, holding on to it would just be a reminder of everything she doesn't want to be reminded of. If she keeps this tiny thing to herself, makes the choice not to tell Ade about it, maybe she'll get a little of her power back.

Decision made, Ife suddenly feels light. She finds herself moving, almost floating into the water, slipping effortlessly past the police tape.

In secondary school, she'd been one of the best in her class at rounders, and even though she hasn't played in years, her pitching skills come in handy now. Back straight, one leg behind the other. Forward. Back. Throw. Ife closes her eyes, and the ring flies free.

When she is back on dry land, Ife remembers the man's parting words and removes the paper he's given her from her pocket. Sure enough, his number is scrawled, almost illegibly, alongside his name.

Mark, the paper reads.

CHAPTER NINE

Three weeks before Cynthia's disappearance

Although the sun was shining brightly through the living-room window, Cynthia was sure she could see thunderclouds gathering as she gave the floor a final hoover before Mama arrived. After over a month of planning, prepping and regretting the fact that she'd agreed to this in the first place, D-Day had finally arrived, and nothing was done.

'Didn't you clean in here already?' Ade was holding Cynthia's favourite cow-shaped mug and staring at her like she'd grown an extra eyebrow. He plonked the mug on the coffee table even though the bloody coaster was sitting *right* there.

Pretending she hadn't heard him, Cynthia went back to hoovering, using more force than was strictly necessary.

'Babe.' Ade wrestled the hoover away from her, switched it off and sat her down on the sofa, passing her the cup of chamomile tea he'd made. 'You need to relax.'

But how could she when it felt like their entire relationship was hanging on the hinges of this weekend? As much as she wanted to tell herself that Mama's opinion didn't matter, she couldn't shake the feeling that it did, far more than Ade let on. So she took a sip of her too-hot tea and forced Ade to go over the plan. Again.

Tonight, after Mama had taken the nap she apparently needed after a long drive, Ade would treat her and Tayo to dinner.

'You sure you don't want to come?'

Cynthia made a face and took another sip of her tea, which was doing nothing to calm her nerves.

'And tomorrow?'

'Spa day for you, tourist day for Mum.' Ade observed her for a moment, contemplating.

'Don't.' Cynthia knew what he was going to say, and she didn't want to hear it. Under no circumstances was she going to spend any more time with Mama than she absolutely had to.

'Fine,' Ade conceded. 'But the sooner you two make up, the easier this is going to be.'

'Yeah, sure.' Cynthia went to take yet another sip of tea, but Ade swiped her mug before she had a chance, this time resting it on the coaster.

'Come here,' he told her, inviting her into a hug. She leant into him, and he wrapped his arms around her, holding her until her breathing slowed to its normal pace.

'I can't wait for this to be over,' he whispered, kissing the sensitive spot behind her ear. His lips made a gentle trail to her collarbone and Cynthia closed her eyes, allowing herself to melt into his touch.

'I've missed this,' he said, releasing the top button of her blouse. His lips made a beeline to her chest, and Cynthia's skin tingled in response. Ever since she'd agreed to Mama's visit, their relationship had been strained, and it felt so good to be close to him again. So good that she found herself sliding into his lap, her lips locking onto his, her arms winding around his neck.

Soon her blouse was on the floor, and Ade was trying and failing to unhook her bra.

'Is this thing new?' he asked her, his expression confused. Cynthia had to bite her lip to keep herself from giggling, and he leant in to kiss her again. Finally, the clasp broke free, and . . .

Knock knock knock.

'Eh-lo?'

Both their heads swivelled to the window where Mama was peering through the open curtain.

Ade swore under his breath and motioned for Cynthia to get down. She crouched by the sofa using her free hand to feel for her blouse on the floor. Ade adjusted himself and went to let Mama in, muttering something about doorbells, while Cynthia threw on her blouse, doing as many buttons as she could in record time.

'You okay?' she heard a voice say, just as she was stuffing her bra down one of the chairs.

She looked up to see Tayo standing in the doorway.

'Yay, you made it.' She stood up to give him a side hug. 'Did you drive up with your mum?'

'Hell, no, I don't have a death wish,' he replied. 'I brought my Mini.'

'Bet that went over great.'

'Yeah, well—' Tayo shrugged.

'Omotayo,' Mama snapped, coming up behind him. 'What are you standing there for? Will you collect the rest of my bags from the car?'

As Tayo left, Ade returned, dragging a pair of Ghana Must Go bags into the living room, the muscles in his arms straining from the effort.

Cynthia pressed her fingers against her temples, trying to force her blood pressure to return to normal. Back when Cynthia was still touring, she'd had a Nigerian roommate with a similar set of bags. *It's the kind of bag you pack when you mean to stay*, the roommate had informed her.

Ade carried them into the kitchen, leaving Cynthia and Mama alone in the living room. Mama's expression was unreadable as she walked towards her, her gold and green traditional wear glaring as she moved.

Seconds ticked by before Mama's expression exploded into the smile usually reserved for her favourite son. She opened her arms and pulled Cynthia into her floral-scented embrace.

At first, Cynthia was shocked and, yes, a little frightened, but after a moment she found herself returning the hug. Behind Mama, Ade was looking pleased with himself.

What did you say to her? Cynthia asked him silently. Ade lifted his palms. *Nothing*, his face replied. *I didn't say a thing.* He reached into the back pocket of his jeans, pulled out his phone and pointed it at them.

Don't you dare.

He grinned and took the photo anyway.

Mama finally let go when Tayo returned.

'Where should I put these?' he asked.

'Put it on my head,' Mama replied, kissing her teeth. 'Adebayo, where is my room?'

Before following Mama upstairs, Ade turned to Tayo.

'Mum and I are going out for dinner tonight,' he said, and it took all of Cynthia's strength not to roll her eyes at him. He sounded like the Beast inviting Belle to sup with him. 'I'd really like it if you came . . . I'll try and keep Mum off your case.'

Tayo looked over at Cynthia, who busied herself by fluffing one of the cushions.

'Yeah, sure,' Tayo said slowly. 'I'll come.'

'Great.' Ade smoothed his wrinkle-free shirt, took the bags Tayo was holding and went to carry them upstairs.

'Is it just me or are those two acting really weird?' Tayo asked.

'Tell me about it,' Cynthia replied. 'Wanna see your room?'

'I get a room?'

Cynthia had turned one of the guest rooms into a bedroom for Tayo, painted it in royal blue and kitted it out with a desk and some new drawers. When she'd told Ade what she was doing, he hadn't seemed too pleased, but thankfully he'd kept his unwanted opinions to himself.

'Ah, so this is why you were asking me all those questions the other week,' he said, admiring a giant poster of his favourite anime characters.

'Do you like it?'

'Yeah, but be honest with me, C.' He paused. 'It was you who put all this together, innit? Not Ade.'

'No,' Cynthia insisted. '*We* thought you might like a home away from home. *We* know how hard it's been, so *we* did this for you.'

Tayo rubbed his eye. 'Okay.'

'Besides,' Cynthia added. 'If you get into Bournemouth, you can live with us and save on rent.'

'Oh, yeah.' Tayo scratched the back of his head and grinned.

'Wait? You got in?'

Tayo nodded.

'Oh my God,' Cynthia squealed and did a little happy dance. Tayo awkwardly joined in.

'When do you start?'

'Late September. Just enough time to practise my "I'm dropping out of med school to follow my dreams" speech.'

'You'll get through it,' Cynthia assured him, patting him on the shoulder. 'And then you'll be free.'

Tayo made a face. 'Just don't tell Ade yet, okay?'

An hour later, Cynthia listened with relief to the crunch of tyres on gravel as Ade drove Mama and Tayo to dinner. She closed her eyes, absorbing the silence, and picked up the book she was reading. It was a self-help book about manifesting your destiny that Mark had recommended. She took a photo of it and posted it on Instagram.

finally some me time, she wrote.

She'd always been an avid Instagrammer, but it was Mark who'd suggested she share her choreography on there too. Since then, her follower count had tripled, old colleagues had reached out to her, and things were finally picking up at the studio. It now seemed silly that she hadn't thought of this before.

Just as she was beginning to settle in, the doorbell rang, and Cynthia slid down on the sofa. Maybe if she kept still whoever it was would go away. The doorbell rang again, followed by relentless knocking. Annoyed, Cynthia threw her book on the seat beside her and went to answer the door.

Mark was waving at her through the peephole.

CHAPTER TEN

Ife, present day

Ade is crying in his sleep again. His violent sobs shake the bed as he says *I'm sorry, I'm sorry, I'm sorry* over and over again. He isn't apologising to her, though, and Ife stares at the darkened ceiling trying to decide if she should wake him.

It hurts to see him like this, to know that he's in so much pain and there's nothing she can do about it – that, in a way, she is to blame. If it wasn't for Cynthia, she wouldn't be here, living in Cynthia's house, lying in Cynthia's bed, wondering if she should be discussing Cynthia's murder with the man Cynthia had apparently turned down.

She knows that she should probably tell him about the text messages and Mark's accusations, but what good would it do? If the past few days are anything to go by, it would only cause him to become more distant than he already is. And she can't risk making things worse, can't risk hurting him even more. She's waited far too long to get here, fought far too hard to have their marriage ruined before it's even started, and with a baby on the way . . . She'll have to deal with Mark and whoever the hell is threatening her on her own.

Still, she can't just sit back and watch the man she loves fall apart, even if it is over another woman.

Resisting the urge to go back to sleep and pretend that she's in the marriage she'd always dreamt of – unmarred by killers and threats and secrets – Ife leans over and places a warm, clammy hand on Ade's bare shoulder. He stills, and the crying stops.

'Dey?' she whispers.

His eyes snap open, and Ife's heart stalls. He stares ahead, his eyes transfixed on the darkness in front of him.

'I know this is hard. But I'm here.' She gives his shoulder a reassuring squeeze, channelling all her compassion, all her guilt, into the gesture.

It is as if he hasn't heard her, hasn't felt her.

How can she be there for him when he won't even talk to her?

Suddenly, he is on his feet.

At first, Ife thinks he's going to the en-suite bathroom, but he walks right past it and makes his way, barefoot and shirtless, through the bedroom door, muttering under his breath.

Determined to push through, Ife slips on her dressing gown and her slippers and follows him down the stairs, past the living room and into the kitchen.

'Do you want a drink?' she asks. 'Some water? Or maybe something stronger?'

As she rifles through the messy cupboards in search of some glasses, an icy wind rustles through the kitchen. Ife turns to find he's opened the door to the garden.

'What are you . . . it's freezing out there.'

Ade doesn't respond, or as Ife now suspects, cannot hear her. He is staring out into the snowy darkness, undisturbed by the cold that has Ife rubbing her covered arms for warmth.

She forgets the glasses, tugs on his arm to pull him back, but somehow he is twice as heavy and doesn't budge.

'Cynthia?'

Ife drops his arm.

Ade steps over the threshold. His feet land gently, leaving footprints as he stalks towards the grass where her belongings are once again scattered. He makes his bed there, trailing his hands across the snow.

Sobbing Cynthia's name.

CHAPTER ELEVEN

Ife, present day

Ife wakes up to a tear-stained pillow and an empty bed.

Earlier, she'd managed to shake Ade awake, had led him upstairs, drawn him a bath and put him back to bed, neither of them saying a word. Once he'd finally fallen back to sleep, she'd pulled Mark's number from under her pillow. When she'd put it there, she'd managed to convince herself she had no intention of using it, but as she held the crumpled paper in her shaking hands, she realised she needed to talk to someone, anyone, who might understand what was going on. Then again, she had no idea if Mark had been telling the truth about his relationship with Cynthia. For all she knew, *he* was the one threatening her. He was also the only one willing to give her answers, and so Ife had forced her reservations aside and sent Mark a message, asking him to meet.

His response had been immediate: 10am, Nyara's café.

Now, as she lies in bed, once again alone, she knows she's made the right decision. Maybe she can't trust Mark, but speaking to him is better than the alternative – doing nothing and waiting for the clock to run out on her marriage. If she can just get through her morning routine, get out of the house to meet with Mark, everything will be okay – she is sure of it.

After her shower, Ife sits at Cynthia's dresser to apply her make-up. She has one just like this in storage, and she allows herself to believe that this one belongs to her.

Step by step, she transforms herself, smoothing away her fears one product at a time. It is not a mask but a mirror, a reflection of how she wants to feel inside.

When she is finally ready, when she has finally created the bold, fearless version of herself she wants to be today, she reaches for her setting powder and leans towards the mirror to apply it.

Cynthia's own perfectly made-up face is staring back at her.

Ife blinks, waves her hand in front of the mirror hoping Cynthia's image will clear, but she remains – lips pursed, her expression judgmental.

All the hurt and anger and guilt Ife has been feeling whirls up inside her, and a distorted voice, the one she's been trying to ignore since Ade's arrest, tells her this is all her fault.

This time she can't dismiss it, can't shake the feeling that maybe it's right.

You did this.

You're the reason she's dead.

It's only a matter of time until they find out the truth.

'Stop. Stop. Stop.'

Ife hurls her powder at the mirror. Spiderwebs appear on the glass, and Cynthia vanishes, replaced by Ife's own fragmented reflection. *Shit.*

Her whole body is shaking now, and Ife takes several deep breaths, trying to calm herself down. Now is not the time to panic. Sort out the mirror, she tells herself. Then go and meet Mark.

She nods.

Drawing on strength she didn't know she had, she turns the vanity so the mirror is facing the wall, prays that Ade will be too distracted to notice and sends Mark a message, asking if they can meet earlier.

As she waits for Mark's response, the sound of laughter, Ade's, catches her attention. She follows it downstairs, past the Cynthia-filled living room and into the kitchen, where she finds Ade sitting alone at the kitchen table, his coffee mug next to him, his phone nowhere in sight. 'I miss you,' he says.

Ife's own phone slips from her hand, landing on the wooden floor with a thud. Ade's head shoots up in surprise.

'Fey?' he says, and for the first time in over a decade, she wishes he hadn't noticed her.

'Morning,' she says, inching into the kitchen. He stands to greet her, brushing invisible dirt from his shorts.

Who were you talking to? she wants to ask.

'How are you this morning?' she asks instead. The words sound strangely formal.

'Fine. Good,' he replies. He's next to her now, and he gives her shoulder a gentle squeeze. Ife wants to hug him. Instead, she decides to be brave.

'Were you on the phone just now?' she asks sweetly, innocently, hopefully not accusingly.

Her careful tone is useless. Ade shifts away from her, and the fraction of warmth she was getting from his body instantly evaporates.

'What are you on about?' he asks. 'My phone's in the living room.' He lifts his hands and shakes his pocketless clothing to emphasise his point.

'I thought I heard you . . .'

Right on cue, his confusion shifts to exasperation. 'If you're going to accuse me of something, why don't you come right out and say it?'

'I wasn't accusing you,' Ife says softly, feeling herself retreat internally. 'I was just . . . asking a question, making conversation.' She sniffs. Between last night and this morning, she can't take any more. It doesn't help that Ade is acting like everything is normal, like she hadn't watched him lying half-naked in the snow, sobbing his ex's name.

'Aw, come on, Fey. Don't cry.'

Ade's hand returns to her shoulder, and his fingernail

catches in a strand of hair. He untangles himself and puts an arm around her.

'You must be tired,' he says, changing the subject. He smiles at her and brushes his fingers over her tummy. 'Maybe it's the hormones or something?'

Surprised, Ife looks up into his crinkling eyes.

'You *know*?'

'Obviously I know,' he tells her. He pulls her into him, and Ife's heart blooms. 'Despite popular belief, I'm not a complete idiot. I notice . . . things.'

'Then why didn't you say something?' Feeling the weight of her secret lifting, she wraps her arms around him.

'Why didn't *you* say something?'

Because she wanted to be sure the baby wasn't the reason he was marrying her, but she isn't about to admit to that, so she shrugs.

'I just couldn't find the right moment.'

'We're going to be parents,' he says. For the briefest moment, he looks as if he wants to kiss her, but then the spell breaks. He jerks away from her as if he's heard something. Seconds later he returns, and again it's like nothing happened.

'Breakfast?' he asks. 'This is meant to be our honeymoon, right? Let me cook you something.'

Ife shakes her head. As much as she wants to spend time with him, if she doesn't speak to Mark soon, she might never have breakfast with him again. 'Actually, I think I'm going to take a walk.'

She waits for him to protest, but he simply shrugs. 'Okay. See you in a bit.' Hiding her disappointment, she pulls on her knee-length jacket, closes the door gently behind her then follows the map on her phone, past Windchapel's wintry hills, until she finds herself outside a café a few metres from the beach.

CHAPTER TWELVE

Three weeks before Cynthia's disappearance

'Nice hat,' Mark said when Cynthia opened the door for him. He'd cut his hair since she'd last seen him, and his already striking eyes stood out even more against his tanned skin.

Cynthia rolled her own eyes and pulled her satin bonnet from her head. 'I thought I told you not to come.'

'I know,' Mark replied. 'But you weren't picking up your phone, so—'

'So you turned up at my house?' Cynthia stared at him in disbelief.

'I know, sorry,' Mark said, rubbing the back of his neck. 'I wouldn't have come if it wasn't important.'

Cynthia sighed. As frustrating as his intrusion was, she was kind of glad to see him.

He must have sensed that she was about to give in because he lifted the pair of M&S bags he was holding. 'I brought food,' he said.

Since she hadn't gone to dinner with the Dolapos, and she wasn't in the mood to cook, she'd planned on ordering a takeaway for one. Free food and Mark's company sounded like a win to her.

'Fine.' Cynthia widened the door to let him in. 'But you can't stay long, Ade will be home soon, and I don't want any drama.'

Over the past two months, Mark had been coming over to help her with promoting the studio, which Ade hadn't been pleased about. He'd met Mark a handful of times, and they hadn't gelled.

'I don't like the way he looks at you,' he'd admitted in a remarkable display of self-awareness.

'How's that?' she'd replied.

'The same way I do when you're wearing your leopard-print yoga pants.'

Cynthia had laughed. 'Don't be silly,' she'd told him. 'You haven't looked at me like that in ages.'

She'd decided it was best not to point out that her working with Mark was no different to him working with Ife, sometimes late into the night, but she hadn't been in the mood to argue, so instead she'd relegated their meetings to the café opposite the studio. If Mark had shown up just five minutes earlier, Cynthia might have had a fight on her hands. As always, his timing was impeccable.

'No drama. Got it.' Mark grinned a grin that was a little too cheeky for her liking and followed her inside. 'In fact, a drama-free night is exactly what I need. Emma's been giving me—'

Mark froze mid-sentence and glanced around the living

room, his expression concerned. 'Something's different,' he said.

'Different how?'

'I don't know,' he said, pacing around the room. 'It just feels different, you know? Like the vibe is off.'

Mark was always going on about vibes and crystals and chakras. While Cynthia had no interest in any of this, she usually humoured him, allowing him to read her aura or lecture her about twin flames.

He came to a stop by the chair she'd stuffed her bra down, and Cynthia jumped in front of him before he had a chance to go digging for treasure.

'Ade's mum was here earlier. Maybe it's that.' She sat in the chair and sent him to the kitchen to get some plates and glasses.

When he returned, they settled down on the living-room floor, and Mark pulled a thermos flask from his bag.

'You cooked?'

'Mac and cheese,' he said, and Cynthia could barely stop herself from drooling. She motioned for the thermos, poured the warm, golden gooeyness onto her plate and lifted it to her nose. *Heaven.*

'Big mac and cheese fan?'

'The biggest.' Cynthia closed her eyes, took a bite and sighed before remembering where she was and who she was with. She looked up to find Mark staring at her, amusement dancing in his eyes.

'Dude, this is amazing, thank you,' she said, stopping just short of telling him he'd made her week. She didn't want him to get too big-headed. 'Seriously, where'd you learn to cook?'

'Actually, I didn't,' he said, uncorking the bottle of wine and filling their glasses. He handed Cynthia a glass and signalled for the thermos. 'I have someone that cooks for me,' he continued.

'Like a personal chef?' *Or a secret lover . . .*

'What can I say? I'm a busy guy.' He held up his glass, and they clinked. 'Besides,' he added, 'I'm still adjusting to the bachelor lifestyle.' His tone was light, but the playfulness in his expression had disappeared.

Cynthia put down her fork. He'd brought her favourite food without even knowing it. The least she could do was listen.

'It must be hard,' she told him. 'Starting a whole new life in the middle of nowhere.' Something Cynthia could definitely relate to.

'Yeah, sometimes . . .'

'What happened with you two, anyway?'

'With me and Emma?'

Cynthia nodded and took a sip of her wine. Despite their growing friendship, Mark hadn't spoken much about his relationship with his soon-to-be-ex-wife, unless he was complaining about their ongoing divorce proceedings.

'Honestly?' He looked away from her, searching for the right words. 'We fell out of love.'

'Was there someone else?'

'It's . . . complicated.'

'Meaning?' In Cynthia's experience, when a man said his relationship was complicated, it was usually code for *I'm a fuckboi*. But maybe this was different. They were married, after all.

'Relax, I didn't cheat.' Mark must have caught her appalled expression. 'You church girls are always jumping to conclusions.'

'Church girls?' Cynthia couldn't remember if she'd told Mark that her father was a pastor, or what had happened with her first serious boyfriend, Francis. 'What's that supposed to mean?' she asked.

'Oh,' Mark said. 'I thought you said you were a Christian? Sorry, I shouldn't have assumed.'

Whether or not she still considered herself a Christian was a can of worms Cynthia did not want to open tonight, despite Mark's curious expression. Obviously, he was deflecting.

'You were saying?' Cynthia said, turning the conversation back on him. 'About not cheating?'

He shrugged. 'I've always believed that if you want to be happy, you have to live honestly. To pursue what you want, no matter the consequences. I couldn't keep living this lie with Emma, so I ended it. *Before* something happened.'

'And where is she now, this woman you gave it all up for?'

It was Mark's turn to drink his wine. He looked pained, like she'd struck a nerve.

'I'm working on it.' He grabbed his backpack. 'In the meantime . . . the reason I came.'

He pulled his laptop from his bag, opened an app and showed it to her. Her eyes widened as she scanned the email.

'You got the investor to come?'

Mark had been reaching out to a few arts investors he knew who might be interested in funding the studio and had invited them to come to her upcoming summer recital.

'*We* did,' he corrected her. 'And *investors*. The two I told you about are both coming. Here, look.' Mark placed his laptop between them, and Cynthia settled in a safe distance away from him. He explained what would happen the night of the show and how it would work if she got the investment.

As the evening rolled on and the wine continued to flow, the conversation shifted to rehearsals, social media and Mark's music. Somehow, they had drifted towards each other, Mark's arm snaked behind her, his hand resting on the floor by her knee.

It took a pair of headlights streaming through the living-room window for Cynthia to realise how close they were now sitting.

'Shit.' Cynthia sprang to her feet, grabbing the plates and glasses then dumping them in the kitchen sink. How had two hours passed so quickly?

When she returned, Mark was still sitting there, watching her like they had all the time in the world.

'Hello . . . Mark?' Cynthia waved her hands in front of his face. 'Come on . . .' she motioned for him to hurry up, but he didn't move.

'This is wrong,' he told her. 'He should trust you.'

He was right – of course he was right – but this was not the time to evaluate the problems in her relationship. The headlights shut off, and Cynthia threw her hands in the air.

'Mark, for God's sake.'

He finally stood, with a sigh. He picked up his laptop and slipped it into his backpack. Then he put his thermos and the bottle of wine into his plastic bag and looked around for his shoes. All the while, he lectured her about how a lack of trust had destroyed his marriage. This from the guy who may or may not have cheated.

A car door slammed, and Cynthia couldn't take it anymore. She grabbed Mark's Crocs, thrust them into his arms and pushed him through the kitchen towards the back door. Mark didn't resist. In fact, he seemed to be enjoying himself.

By the time they got to the back door, his mood seemed to have sobered. He looked down at her.

'Stay safe, okay?' he told her before, at long last, he disappeared into the night.

The front door opened behind her, and Cynthia rushed back to the living room.

'What are you doing up?' Ade leant down to kiss Cynthia's forehead. 'I thought you'd be in bed by now.'

'I, uh, couldn't sleep.'

She looked behind Ade and Tayo, hoping that their towering statures were concealing Mama's tiny frame.

'Where's your mum?' she asked, trying to hide the panic in her voice.

Ade rolled his eyes. 'She said she wants to pray over the garden before she goes to bed.'

Cynthia closed her eyes, trying to stay calm. She opened her mouth to speak, but her tongue had stopped working, so she closed it again.

'What's wrong?'

Cynthia winced. 'Mark came by to—'

Ade's concern flipped into fury. 'I don't believe this—'

'Ade,' Mama interrupted, and Cynthia turned to find her gripping a cowering Mark by his ear. 'What is this Oyinbo boy doing in your garden?'

CHAPTER THIRTEEN

Ife, present day

When Ife pushes open the café's frosted-glass door, she immediately feels like she's stepped into a bag of M&Ms. Red, yellow and blue chairs are scattered in no particular pattern across the empty room, and the entire place smells like chocolate with a hint of coffee. Harlem Renaissance-style paintings of sax players and jazz dancers hang on the wall, but it's the hi-fi system with headphones and CDs stacked on high that catches Ife's attention.

The collection is as eclectic as the café itself, and Ife rifles through it – through Usher and Nirvana, Destiny's Child and My Chemical Romance – until she spots that unmistakable black-and-gold cover.

It used to be her favourite album, but for years she hasn't been able to bring herself to listen to it. Today is different, though. Today she wants to remember, and so she slips the CD into place and skips to Track 8, the same track they'd played at her Year 11 prom.

Demi had forced her to go. If it had been up to her, she would have stayed at home in her pyjamas eating Chilli Heatwave Doritos and watching black-and-white horror movies. Maybe then she wouldn't have agreed to go with Jamal, the guy from sixth form, who'd been trying to chat her up in the library and whom she was slowly starting to like.

Even though she hadn't wanted to go, Jamal had done his best to make the evening special. Had brought her a pink rose when he'd picked her up from Demi's house and hadn't seemed to mind when she'd stepped on his toes as they danced. Instead, he'd held her more tightly, the smell of Lynx Africa making her insides go all warm and tingly. She'd been resting her cheek against his shoulder when Ade had cut in and asked to speak to her alone.

As Joe's 'No One Else Comes Close' played in the background, he'd told her how amazing she looked, how tired he was of boarding school and Chantelle.

'I miss you, Fey,' he'd said, the tip of his nose brushing against hers. If the crowd hadn't erupted when Tiny Stitches, the act for the night, bounced onto stage, Ife knew what would have happened next. Instead, Ade had slipped away to find his actual girlfriend, and a hurt Jamal had told her she was wasting her time with a wasteman like Ade.

Demi had been pissed off, too. Jamal was meant to be their ride home, and she, too, was fed up with her Ade drama.

'You need to cut him loose, Fey,' she'd told her. 'Don't let no man mess up your life.'

Instead of apologising, Ife had left early and walked

home alone. She knew Demi was right. Knew Ade was bad for her. Why did she have to love him so much?

Later that night, while she was in bed watching *The Birds* on her portable DVD player, Ade had called. At first, she hadn't picked up. She had no interest in speaking with him ever again. But when her phone rang a third, a fourth and then a fifth time, her resolve crumbled.

'What?' she'd said before he had a chance to say hello or apologise.

'You haven't heard?' he asked. He'd sounded upset, really upset, and Ife sat up, her heart suddenly pounding. 'What's happened?'

There'd been an accident. Jamal had been driving Demi and a few others home when they'd collided with another car. There was speculation that the drinks at the dance had been spiked. That Jamal or the other driver had been drunk.

'I'm sorry, Fey,' Ade had said gently through the phone. 'Jamal, Demi – they didn't make it.'

Ife hadn't realised her phone had fallen from her hands until Ade was in her room, holding her as she sobbed into his shoulder.

'This is all my fault,' she'd whispered. If she hadn't hurt Jamal's feelings, hadn't left Demi behind, none of this would have happened. She was a bad friend, a terrible person. She didn't deserve Ade's comfort, or friendship. She didn't deserve Ade's love. No wonder he'd run away from her.

'Hey,' Ade had said. 'Look at me.'

She met his eyes, filled with so much care and concern it made her want to start crying all over again.

'This isn't your fault,' he'd told her, and she turned away, unable to accept his words.

'Hey.' He placed his hand over hers. It was warm and soft. 'Look at me,' he said again.

She did. His face was blurry from behind her tears, and she couldn't make out his expression.

'You can't blame yourself for this,' he'd whispered. 'You don't want to carry that. Trust me.'

Ife nodded, remembering that he had a similar cross to bear.

'We're going to get through this,' he'd told her. 'Everything's going to be okay.'

To this day, Ife doesn't understand why she did what she did next. Maybe it was the grief, or the guilt, or the gratefulness. Maybe it was the way he was holding her hand or the fact that in that moment she needed him more than she'd ever needed anyone. Whatever the reason, she'd found herself shifting even closer to him as she entwined her fingers with his.

'Girl, no,' she heard Demi's voice say, but Demi had left her all alone, hadn't given her a choice. She didn't get a say in this. And so she'd moved closer and closer and closer to him until their lips were almost touching, just like at prom.

Except this time, Ade had shot like a bullet from the bed, as far away as he could get from her in one swift move.

'Woah . . . Fey.' His hands were in the air, then on his head. 'Woah.'

'I thought . . .' Ife had blinked, shocked by her actions, stunned by his response.

'We can't . . .' He was rubbing his forehead like he was trying to erase the memory from his mind. 'You thought . . . We're friends . . . I . . .' He'd stopped talking when Ife had dived under her covers and shielded her face with her duvet.

Long, silent seconds ticked by, and then, 'Fey?'

Ife didn't respond. She wanted him to go away so she could get used to being alone.

'Ife.'

Again, Ife kept quiet, and moments later she heard his soft footsteps on the carpet. Her door shutting gently behind him.

CHAPTER FOURTEEN

Three weeks before Cynthia's disappearance

Cynthia couldn't sleep.

Earlier, Ade had managed to explain away Mark's presence by claiming he was just an eccentric neighbour who liked to roam the village at night and sometimes found himself in other people's gardens. He was a bit weird, Ade had told Mama, but generally harmless.

Cynthia had thought Mama wouldn't believe them, but apparently she did, because she'd launched into her own monologue about a similar man who roamed around her village back in Nigeria. She mentioned how her late husband, Ade's father, had often struck up conversations with the man, whom he claimed was not mad at all but had a unique perspective of the world.

It was the first time Cynthia had heard Mama, or anyone else for that matter, speak about Ade's father, other than in passing. Ade usually avoided the subject altogether, and, as Mama's story unfolded, Tayo had listened intently while Ade glared at Cynthia, the vein on his forehead throbbing. Even though he'd covered for her, she knew this was far from over. She remembered Mark's warning about trust and shifted in her seat.

'You know what?' Ade had stomped to his feet. 'I'm going to bed.' He'd stormed out of the living room without even looking at Cynthia. Cynthia mumbled goodnight to Mama and Tayo before rushing after him.

'I'm sorry,' she'd said, once they were safely in their bedroom. 'He had something important to show me, that's all.'

No response as Ade rummaged through the cupboards for a spare pillow and blanket.

'Baby, please,' she said, placing her hand on his shoulder. His whole body stiffened. She'd forgotten how much he hated being touched when he was angry. She quickly stepped back, rushing towards their bedroom door to keep him from leaving.

She couldn't bear to end the night like this, to leave him thinking the worst of her.

'Why don't you trust me?' she asked him.

He looked at her with an expression she couldn't quite read. There was anger there, of course, disappointment too, but there was also something else. Something she had never seen in him before.

'Move.'

Several silent seconds ticked by. Cynthia's heart was beating so hard she could no longer hear her thoughts. She knew she should do as he was asking, but her feet were stuck.

'Ade,' she pleaded, her voice weak and shaky.

Ade took a step forward, so close they were almost touching. For a moment, she was sure he was going to move her himself. If he did, it would be over.

'Cynthia.' His tone was filled with warning. His fists were clenched, and he was shaking.

She stared at him, silently begging him to just listen to what she had to say. His expression remained stony, and Cynthia knew better than to push him further.

She stepped out of his way, and he stormed out of the room, brushing her chin with his shoulder as he passed her.

Now, hours later, unable to sleep, Cynthia shoved her duvet away from her and dragged herself out of bed. Across the corridor, Tayo's light was still on.

'You couldn't sleep either?' Cynthia asked him, poking her head around the door to find him at his desk, drawing.

'Yeah, Mum and Ade woke me up with their arguing, and I haven't been able to get back to sleep.'

'Really?' Cynthia paused to listen, and, sure enough, she could hear their raised voices below, although she couldn't quite make out what they were saying. Tayo's room was above the living room, which was probably why he'd heard them and she hadn't. 'What are they fighting about?'

'You, I think.'

'Wonderful.'

'Sorry,' he said, looking up from his canvas. 'If it helps, it sounds like he's defending you.'

'What are you working on?' Cynthia asked, not wanting Tayo to get involved in their row.

'It's for you, actually.' He shifted his elbow so she could take a closer look. 'I used one of the photos you sent me.'

He'd drawn her beloved boat with startling accuracy, perfectly capturing the way the sun made its blue stripes sparkle and the quiet chaos of the harbour.

'It's beautiful.'

'Pass me that frame over there, please.'

Cynthia took the frame from a shelf behind her and gave it to him. He signed the corner of the picture, placed it carefully in the frame and held it out to her.

'This is so sweet, thank you,' Cynthia said, trying to keep herself from tearing up. Although Ade was mad at her, she was touched by the fact that both Tayo and Mark were looking out for her.

'Now,' she said, coughing her tears away. 'I'm going to the kitchen to get some water. Want anything?'

Tayo raised his eyebrows at her. 'You know eavesdropping is a sin, right?'

'Well, as far as I'm concerned, it is my right as your mother to say whatever I like,' Mama said as Cynthia came to a stop outside the living room. 'She is a useless girl who will only dabaru your life.'

'What about you, Mum? What about the lives *you've* ruined?' Even in the dim light, Cynthia could tell that Ade's rage hadn't subsided. Except now, thankfully, it was being directed at Mama. 'Or you think you can get away with the lies you told about Dad?'

'And so?' Mama sat on the arm of the sofa behind her. 'What has that got to do with any of it?'

Ade crossed his arms. 'You want me to go and wake Tayo up and tell him the truth about what he was really like? About what we did?'

'You see.' Mama clicked her fingers in triumph. 'You see what that woman is doing to us already, and you haven't even married.'

'Yeah well, that's going to change soon.'

Cynthia waited for the inevitable bubble of excitement at the prospect of Ade proposing to her, but it didn't arrive. How could he possibly be thinking about marriage when their relationship was so obviously in crisis?

'Over her dead body.' Mama stood again, circling her hands over her head.

For a moment, all Cynthia could hear was the sound of the clock ticking over the fireplace. When Ade finally spoke, his voice was measured. Cold.

'I've given you your options,' he said. 'So you can

either do as I say' – he paused – 'or you can get the fuck out of my house.'

'If I . . .' Mama's hand was braced for a slap.

Ade gave her a look that said *try me*, and Mama's hand swiftly connected with his cheek, landing with a clap. Ade didn't flinch.

'Like I said . . . you can either do as I say, or fuck off. I won't let you ruin this for me.'

CHAPTER FIFTEEN

Ife, present day

'Excuse me, darling.'

Ife wipes away her tears and hits pause on the song she's now played through half a dozen times. She looks up to find a brightly dressed woman leaning over her with a large yellow mug. Long golden earrings dangle from her lobes, and a chunky beaded necklace hangs around her neck, almost touching Ife's nose. None of what she's wearing seems to match, and yet, somehow, she still looks radiant.

'It's decaf.' She hands Ife the mug and settles on the edge of her chair.

'I'm Nyara, by the way.' Her smile is so warm that Ife can't help but smile back. 'I've never seen you around here before.'

'I'm new to the area,' Ife admits, unsure of how much she should give away, of how much Nyara has heard. 'I just got married.' She waits for Nyara to connect the dots, to realise she's seen Ife's photo in the paper or online, but instead she smiles again.

'Oh, well, congratulations.' The lilt of her Trini accent gives way in her excitement. 'I see why you're so tired now.

New home, new husband, a little one on the way. I still remember how exhausted I was when I was expecting my Winston.'

Ife sips her coffee, trying to mask her surprise. She's spent all this time hiding her pregnancy, but apparently it was obvious to everyone. It's a relief to know she doesn't have to hide anymore but also odd that a stranger guessed so easily. Maybe she's showing more than she thought.

'I have an eye for these things.' Nyara pats Ife's shoulder. 'Though Lord knows this is no place to raise a child anymore. It used to be so peaceful here. A little slow in the off-season, not many people that look like us, but still, I felt happy here. Safe.'

She glances up at the TV, where a photograph of Cynthia in a bikini smiling seductively into the camera appears on the screen. Nyara kisses her teeth.

'They tryna make it seem like she had it coming,' she says. 'But she was a nice girl.'

Ife sits up. 'You knew her?'

Nyara nods. 'She owned the dance studio just across the street there.' She motions behind her. 'She'd come in here to work on her business plan, and we'd get to talking. Girl never had a licka business sense, God rest her soul, but she was nice. Sweet. I knew something happened when she stopped coming in, but . . .' Nyara's voice cracks, and she sniffs.

'Any idea what might have happened to her?' Ife asks, reaching up to place a gentle hand on Nyara's arm.

Nyara glances around her empty café, then leans in. 'I know she was having trouble with she boyfriend,' she tells her. 'She moved into the apartment above the studio to get away from him. Boy was not happy, I can tell you that.'

'Did she say why?'

Nyara eyes her suspiciously.

'I, uh, read something about it online.'

'Well, I'm not one to gossip.' Nyara fiddles with her necklace. 'But let's just say she wasn't living up there by herself.'

'She was seeing someone else?' Ife swallows, suddenly feeling ill. Mark had apparently been telling the truth about his relationship with Cynthia. And if he was telling the truth about that . . .

Nyara shrugs. 'I don't think she was cheating on her man if that's what you're implying,' she says. 'But she and that white boy were close. He was always in here, telling her how to run her business, giving advice, but from what I heard him saying, he was just as clueless as she.'

As if on cue, Ife's phone vibrates in her bag, and she finds several messages from Mark.

Sorry I missed this, the first one says in response to her request to meet earlier. My flat's across the street. Up the stairs. Red door.

Still coming? the second one asks.

Ife?

Ife downs the rest of her coffee.

'Thank you,' she says. 'But I've got to go.'

'Hold on,' Nyara says, and Ife tenses, worried that Nyara has finally recognised her. Instead, she heads to the till, and returns with a flyer.

'We're having a memorial for Cynthia,' she says, handing it to her. 'You should come.'

'Oh' – Ife shakes her head – 'I don't think . . .'

'Everyone from the village will be there,' Nyara reassures her. 'Most of them didn't know her either. You'll be fine.'

Ife takes the flyer and tucks it into her jacket, pays for her coffee and heads across the street.

Mark's door is unlocked, but the only sign of him is a half-empty coffee mug sitting on the kitchen table. The kitchen's wooden cupboards and shiny white countertops remind her of the luxury apartments she'd stayed at in Dubai. A set of keys sits in a carved wooden bowl along with a few crystals. He can't have gone far without his keys, so Ife makes her way into the living room, where the luxury theme continues with wooden floors and cream sofas, the citrus scent suggesting that the apartment has just been cleaned.

A fluffy grey rug reminds Ife of the one at the house, and

she wonders how long Cynthia lived here. Clearly long enough for her to decorate.

On the other side of the room, there's an electric fireplace with framed photos resting on the mantelpiece. Ife picks up one of Cynthia and Mark, arms linked, smiling at each other. Mark looks bigger here, his arms more muscular, his skin more tan. There is something strangely familiar about these photos, and Ife examines the one in her hand trying to place it, knowing that there's no way she could have seen it before.

Maybe Nyara was right about Mark and Cynthia. They certainly look close in these photos. And yet, something doesn't quite add up. At some point between Cynthia and Ade's breakup and Cynthia's disappearance, Cynthia had started seeing Mark publicly enough for there to be evidence of it, and yet, according to Ade, she'd disappeared soon after they'd ended things. Unless Cynthia *had* been cheating. Either that, or Ade had lied to her about what had happened. But why would he lie?

The image of Ade standing outside her old flat, drunk and upset, flashes in her mind, and she immediately pushes it away. It has nothing to do with this.

She places the photo in her hand back on the mantelpiece and picks up another one.

'That one's my favourite,' a voice behind her says.

CHAPTER SIXTEEN

Ife, present day

Ife almost drops the picture she's holding. Mark slides it from her hands and places it back on the mantelpiece. He's fresh from a shower, his damp wavy hair resting on the towel around his neck.

'Sorry to keep you waiting,' he says. 'I wasn't sure if you were still coming so I hopped in the shower.' He scrunches his hair with the towel, seeming more relaxed compared to the last time she'd seen him, the grief he'd worn so openly barely visible now.

'Here, let me take your coat – you must be boiling in that.'

Ife shakes her head, but she can see why Cynthia had liked him now. Yes, he's handsome, in a lanky green-eyed hipster kind of way. But even more than that: he's perceptive, accommodating, exuding an air of well-tamed confidence which could easily look like arrogance on someone less charming.

'Can I get you something to drink?' he asks, guiding her towards the sofas. 'Coffee?' His eyes drop to her well-hidden tummy. 'Or maybe tea? Cynthia loved chamomile.'

Ife glares at him, but he doesn't seem to notice. 'I'm fine,' she tells him. 'Thank you.'

'Okay.' Mark settles into the chair opposite her. There's a moment of uncomfortable silence before he speaks again. 'You said you had something important to ask me? That it was urgent?'

Ife had thought long and hard about how she could ask Mark about the text messages, about the break-ins, about the possibility of Cynthia still being alive, without sounding like she'd lost her mind. But now that she's here, now that she's spoken to Nyara and seen where he and Cynthia lived, her well-rehearsed speech sticks in her throat, and something else, something more pressing, takes its place.

'You said your relationship with Cynthia was complicated.'

'It was.'

'I guess I was just wondering what you meant by that?' Ife hates how unsure she sounds, a feeling that only intensifies as Mark observes her.

'Before Cynthia came into my life,' he finally says, his voice almost a whisper, 'it was like I had this half-finished melody playing in my head, all the time, on a constant loop. No matter who I was with or how hard I tried, I could never find the right notes to finish the song. To make me whole. And then I met Cynthia.'

He doesn't need to complete the metaphor for Ife to

understand what he's trying to tell her. It's a feeling she's all too familiar with. Except . . .

'Did she feel the same way?'

Mark narrows his eyes. 'What do you think?'

'I think she was in a relationship.'

'With a guy who's now married to someone else.'

He has her there, but Ife presses on. 'So you and Cynthia fall in love, she . . . breaks up with Ade?' She phrases this as a question, looks up at Mark to gauge his reaction, but he isn't giving anything away. 'She moves in with you, and then . . . ?'

'And then, one day, she doesn't come home.'

The silence has returned, thick and heavy with accusation. His eyes stay trained on hers, daring her to defend the indefensible. But she can't, not if she wants his help.

'And when exactly did this happen?' she asks.

Mark pulls his legs towards him, his eyes clouding over. 'The fifteenth of August,' he says. 'The night before her recital. I'd cooked her dinner but she didn't turn up. Naturally, I tried to get in touch with your husband, but . . .'

The fifteenth of August. The room begins to spin, and Mark's voice gets further and further away, replaced by the sound of Ade banging on her front door.

Fey, please let me in.

His eyes were red and wild, his breath laced with rum.

'What's happened?'

'Nothing. I . . . I just miss you.'

'Are you okay?' Mark asks, and Ife slams the door on the unbidden memory.

She's here to protect her marriage not investigate her husband. She's known him her whole life. He isn't capable of what the world is accusing him of.

Besides, if he *had* done it, if he *is* still a suspect, why haven't the police arrested him again? All they need is a body, right?

'No,' she says, shaking her head, deciding to change the subject. 'Someone's been threatening me.'

'And you think it's me?'

'I . . . I don't know.'

She tells him about the break-ins, Cynthia's belongings scattered across the living room, the anonymous text messages.

His expression is stoic. 'Can I see them?'

He seems genuine. Either he's an incredibly talented actor or he isn't the one threatening her.

Ife takes her phone from her bag, opens the messages, and hands it over to Mark, bracing herself for the questions she knows he's going to ask. She knows if he finds out the truth he might not help her, and she'll be back to square one. But what choice does she have? If she wants answers, she might have to tell him what happened. Better Mark than Ade. Maybe if she explains that it is all a misunderstanding, that Cynthia had chosen Mark and Ade had chosen her, and nothing she'd done had caused any of this to happen, he'll be willing to help her find out who is doing this.

She watches as he reads the messages. His expression turns from curious to confused.

'What does this mean?' he asks, pointing at the phone. 'I know what you did. What exactly did you do?'

'Nothing.' Ife shrugs. 'It's just a misunderstanding.'

'It can't be nothing, or you wouldn't be here. Besides, this person sounds *pissed*.'

'Do you know anyone who might have got the wrong idea about me and Ade?' Ife asks, once again dodging the question. 'Who might think I had something to do with what happened? Maybe a close friend of Cynthia's, or a relative?'

'No,' Mark shakes his head. 'Cynthia didn't really have any friends here, and her family are miles away in Manchester. There's only one person I can think of, and . . . well, she's . . .'

His eyes darken, and he looks down, studying the frills on the rug. Eventually, he looks up again and leans forward to hand Ife her phone.

'If I were you,' he says gently. 'I'd get the hell away from that house and that husband of yours. Whatever this is, it's not something you want to be messing with.'

CHAPTER SEVENTEEN

Three weeks before Cynthia's disappearance

'What time are you picking me up?' Cynthia asked as Ade pulled into the car park of the spa he'd booked for her back when she was the one mad at him.

Ade hadn't said a word to her all morning. He'd made a show of kissing her forehead when she'd come down for breakfast, and she'd been foolish enough to believe that he'd forgiven her, that it wasn't just for his mother's benefit.

An hour later, as he drove her to the spa, she'd tried to apologise again, but he'd just stared blankly through the windscreen, pretending she didn't exist.

'You don't trust me,' she'd said, echoing Mark's words as he pulled into a parking space to drop her off. He'd continued to ignore her, tapping his fingers against the steering wheel until she had no choice but to leave.

She knew that he was being childish, that she should have been upset with him too. And yet, she couldn't shake the feeling that she was in the wrong.

Of course, Ade was blowing things way out of proportion since there was absolutely nothing going on with her and Mark at all. But she'd still invited him into their home, fully aware of the potential consequences. Why?

It wasn't a question she was ready to answer, and she hoisted her purple duffle bag onto her shoulder and walked along the wooden path towards the timber lodge that housed Wild Cherry Spa. Usually, she would have stopped to admire the scenery, to take in the man-made lake enveloped by the trees that gave the spa its name. Instead, she rushed towards the building, trying to outpace the guilt threatening to surface.

Inside, the receptionist, bleached blonde with professionally tanned skin, smiled a little too widely when she approached the desk. She was furiously chewing on her gum, and Cynthia half expected it to fall out of her mouth and onto the polished marble desk. An unexpected bubble of laughter escaped from Cynthia's lips at the image, and the woman looked up at her, her composure slipping for a moment before she confirmed Cynthia's details and asked her to take a seat.

Embarrassed, Cynthia made her way to a row of brown leather sofas and watched as an eclectic mix of people walked around the foyer, many of them couples, arm in arm, whispering in each other's ears.

Ade, bless him, would have felt so out of place here. Back when they lived in London, she'd tried to get him to join her for a couples massage, but he'd refused. Apparently, the thought of *some strange woman rubbing oils all over him* gave him the creeps. *Besides,* he'd added, pulling her into him, *we could probably do the same thing right here with way better results.*

This had led to an ill-fated seduction attempt that had landed Ade in A&E. Thankfully, the burns were only minor, and it was something they joked about now. Or *had* joked about. Cynthia was struggling to remember the last time they'd joked about anything.

With a sigh, she returned to her people-watching. A tall man with tightly woven dreadlocks tied back in a ponytail caught Cynthia's eye as he walked in through the automatic doors and made his way across the lobby towards the reception desk. The receptionist's face lit up when she saw him, and Cynthia smiled as they embraced each other. His lanky frame and warm demeanour reminded her of Mark. Like him, Mark was at ease wherever he went – whether they were working at Nyara's café or eating dinner in her living room, he just seemed to *fit*. It made her feel like she fit too.

Add in the fact that he was basically her only friend here, that he seemed to know her so well, and it made sense that she wanted to spend time with him. It didn't mean what Ade thought it meant though, and he had no reason to be jealous. Because, despite everything, it was Ade she wanted to be with. Why couldn't he see that?

'Cynthia?'

Cynthia looked up to find the last person in the universe she wanted to see standing in front of her, her expensive navy tracksuit and glowing skin reminding her of how little she'd slept and how scruffy she must look. Even her hot-pink trainers, with white stripes and three diamantés encrusted on each arch, seemed to be mocking her with their sparkles.

'Ife, right?' she asked, though there was no mistaking that this flawless woman was the same one she'd been forced to endure dinner with a couple of months back.

'Yes,' Ife nodded. 'But you can call me Fey if you want. Ade does.' She tucked an invisible strand of hair behind her ear, and Cynthia tried not to roll her eyes. Pushing away the bubbles of irritation brewing just below the surface, she plastered what she hoped was a friendly smile on her face and asked Ife what had brought her to this particular spa on this fine Saturday morning.

'Actually, a friend of mine recommended it,' Ife replied. 'Apparently, I look like I'm in desperate need of a facial.'

Ife laughed, and Cynthia's smile faltered. She didn't need a psychology degree to figure out who this seemingly insightful friend was, and all the guilt she'd been feeling earlier flew through the spa's automatic doors. Clearly, he was using Ife to try and get back at her, and she refused to participate in his immature mind games.

'Right,' Cynthia said. She stood to her feet just as a

disembodied voice called her name. Relieved to escape their non-conversation, she waved at the woman dressed in the spa's chocolate-brown tunic, who finally spotted her. Tablet in hand, she approached them.

'Cynthia?' Her voice had dropped to a near whisper. 'Ready for your facial?'

Cynthia nodded and turned to pick up her bag. 'It was nice seeing you, Ife.' She smiled sweetly, hoping the fact that she was dancing inside wasn't visible on her face.

'Yeah, nice seeing you too,' she replied, a note of disappointment in her voice. 'Maybe we can catch up later?'

'You can stay together if you want,' the woman said, glancing down at her tablet. 'What did you say your name was?'

'Oh . . . umm—' Cynthia began.

'Ife. Ife Ojo,' Ife interrupted.

'Found you.' The woman tapped on her screen. 'All sorted,' she said, grinning up at them as if she'd done her good deed for the day.

They walked in uncomfortable silence as Cynthia tried to work up the nerve to point out the employee's mistake. Ife seemed more than happy to go along with the plan, and Cynthia was beginning to wish she'd stayed at home. Spending the day tactfully avoiding Mama had to be better than this.

She glanced over at Ife. She couldn't tell if she was

naively oblivious to the role she was playing in her relationship, or if something more sinister was going on. The fact that she and Ade were now working together didn't help, but she had to trust Ade, just like he needed to trust her with Mark.

'Here we are.' The attendant led them into a softly lit room, with dark-brown and cream coloured walls. Notes of vanilla and caramel rose from a nearby candle, while lo-fi music played from invisible speakers.

As they waited for the aesthetician, Cynthia tried her hardest to relax, but Ife breathing next to her only brought her thoughts back to Ade. Their once-fiery relationship had cooled to a near-uncomfortable tepidness, both of them afraid that their next fight would be their last. She'd tried to reignite the conversation they'd had on her boat, to get Ade to open up about his mother. All she knew so far was that it had something to do with his late father, but that was as far as she'd got before he'd told her to back off.

Since his argument with Mama the night before, it had become glaringly obvious that she didn't know her man at all.

It was easy – too easy sometimes – to push these feelings away, especially when he walked into a room with that big goofy smile of his. Especially when he'd take her hand and tell her, in no uncertain terms, that he loved her.

Relief would cloak her previous feelings of despair, and the cycle would start all over again. Except this time the cycle was taking a different route. Now, the warmth that once drew her back into him had frozen over, and it felt like there was no way through.

Mark, on the other hand, had become her blanket. He was always there when she needed him most with a comforting word, or a song he knew she'd like. It was almost uncanny how much they had in common, the same taste in music and movies and food. It might have been a little creepy if she didn't like him so much. Not *like* like, obviously. But he was a likeable guy, anyone could see that.

Anyone except Ade.

Cynthia looked over at Ife who'd just been showing the aesthetician something on her phone and was now sitting back, ankles crossed, as she flipped through the treatment brochure.

Maybe it was the same for her and Ade. Maybe, like her, Ade needed a friend who was separate from their relationship, someone else he could be himself with.

She'd been harbouring a grudge ever since Mama's joke of a dinner, but it wasn't Ife's fault her childhood friend was a coward when it came to his mother. There was no reason they couldn't be cordial. It would at the very least prove to Ade that he was being unfair about Mark.

The aesthetician returned with a bottle of Prosecco, and Ife swung her long legs over the lounger so she was facing Cynthia.

'Thought this might help us relax a bit.' Ife poured them a glass each and went to take a sip.

'Wait.' Cynthia said. She lifted her glass.

'What are we toasting?' Ife asked, raising her glass to meet Cynthia's and reminding Cynthia of Mark the night before, wine glass in hand, green eyes sparkling as he smiled at her.

'To friendship,' Cynthia said, and Ife tilted her head to the side, the trace of a smile brushing her lips.

'To friendship.'

CHAPTER EIGHTEEN

Ife, present day

On the morning of her twelve-week scan, Ife is in the storage cupboard trying to work up the courage to go through Cynthia's things. She's meant to be cooking breakfast for Ade, but when she'd heard him go into the bathroom to shower for the first time since his arrest, she'd turned down the fire on his oats and slipped into the storeroom to begin her search.

Since meeting with Mark, Ife has barely had a moment to herself. Ade has been hovering over her, whispering to her tummy one moment, staring blankly into space the next. Whenever she'd get up to leave whatever room they were in, he'd either follow her out or grab her hand and beg her not to leave him.

Under normal circumstances, she would have relished the fact that he was paying her so much attention. But with the threatening messages becoming more and more frequent and Cynthia's memory lingering over every room in the house, she's found herself pulling away from him, even though she too is desperate for closeness. She knows she needs to uncover the truth.

Now Ife stands frozen with fear, afraid of what she might find and of what might happen if she doesn't look. Maybe she should take Mark's advice, follow the instructions in the messages and just leave. But if she does, if she walks away from this marriage, everything she has been through will have been for nothing.

Besides, if, by some miracle, she's able to find out what happened to Cynthia the night she disappeared, she might be able to save Ade too.

Either that, or she'll find something that incriminates him.

No. Ife shakes the thought from her mind. She won't find evidence against Ade because there is no evidence *to* find. Like her, he had nothing to do with what happened to Cynthia. The sooner she can prove that, the sooner they can get back to living their lives.

And so she takes a deep breath, knowing that this is her only chance to stop Ade from finding out the truth, and lifts the lid on the nearest box.

Inside are papers, books and other trinkets, remnants of the life Cynthia was trying to build with Ade.

Ife begins with a folder of papers: Cynthia's lease for the studio, a business plan, a few printed emails from someone named Janine with information about the building.

She puts them to one side, pretends she hasn't seen the blue-and-white purse tucked into the corner of the box and picks up a book on digital marketing. *You've got this babe x* the inscription in Ade's handwriting reads. Ife claps the book shut, dismissing the pang of jealousy, and drops it on the paperwork. She peers inside the box again, and that's when she spots it, sticking out from under another one of Cynthia's business books.

She tugs at the girl with the Afro and discovers a curved key hanging on the end of it. She turns it over in her hand, back and forth, back and forth, back and . . .

'Ife, will you get up here?' Ade's voice is loud, angry, and she starts, gripping the door handle for support. She'd been clinging to the hope that the threats wouldn't become real for a while, but apparently whoever was stalking her was in a hurry to ruin her life.

Her head light, her heart thumping in her chest, Ife slowly makes her way upstairs. Ade screams her name again just as she's entering the doorway. She can feel his anger bouncing off the walls towards her. She wants to run, knows that the moment she goes in it will be over for them. She can't bear the thought of him hating her, of the look of disdain he'll give her when she tries to explain. But, like Mark had said, her only other option is to leave and not look back, something she isn't willing to do.

She steps into the bedroom and finds him sitting on the edge of their bed. His head is in one hand, and his other hand is in the air, balled into a shaking fist.

'Where did you get this?' He doesn't even lift his head to look at her.

'Dey, what's wrong?'

He doesn't respond. Instead, he opens his clasped hand to show her something.

Confused, she inches towards him to get a closer look, but when she reaches out to take it, he snatches it back before she can even catch a glimpse.

'Where did you get this from?' he asks again, his tone low, his voice shaky.

'Ade.' She sits next to him, hoping he can't see that she's sweating. 'I honestly don't know what you're talking about. Maybe if you tell me what it is, I can give you an answer.'

He finally looks at her, and she sees the same terror in his eyes that was there on their wedding night.

He opens his hand again and reveals a ring. It's almost an exact replica of the one on Ife's finger, except instead of emerald green, the gemstones are a blue-grey, the same colour as the English Channel on a frosty winter morning.

She tries and fails to mask her horrified surprise from Ade, who is watching her intently, awaiting her reaction.

'I don't understand,' she says, her mind asking *how how how how how is this even possible?* Maybe she'd imagined Mark giving her the ring that morning, but even as she thinks it, she knows that can't be it. The text messages from

Mark prove that. She knows, too, that she'd thrown that very ring into the sea, had definitely not brought it home with her, and even if someone *had* found it, how would they have known where to return it? How would they have got into the house to put it in their bedroom for Ade to find? It makes no sense. So how, then? How?

'For fuck's sake, Ife, stop lying.' Ade startles her out of her thoughts. 'Tell me where you got it.'

'I . . .' Self-preservation at last kicks in, and Ife pulls her own ring from her finger and drops it in Ade's hand next to Cynthia's.

'They're almost exactly the same,' she says, the hurt she'd pushed away when Mark had given her the ring resurfacing. 'So you tell me.'

When he doesn't respond, she continues. 'I'm guessing it was Cynthia's?'

Still no answer.

'You proposed to her.'

Ade sighs, closing his eyes. 'Yes.'

'And then you proposed to me.'

'Come on, Fey.' His hand is on her knee now, and it takes all her strength not to shift away from him. 'You know it wasn't like that.'

Does she? All this time she'd been worrying about her mistakes, worrying about hurting him, and he hadn't given a single thought to how this would make her feel. In fact, up until a few moments ago, he was in the process of blaming her for something that was entirely his fault.

'Okay,' she says, slipping her mask back on. 'But I still don't understand why you're acting like this.'

'I came out of the shower, and it was on the bed,' he says carefully. 'I thought, I don't know, maybe you put it there.'

'Why would I—'

'I know.' He cuts her off. 'When I proposed . . .' He glances at Ife. 'When we broke up, I told her to keep it, and I haven't seen it since. It doesn't make sense.'

It's Ife's turn to stay silent. Again, she's reminded of Mark's accusations, about the fact that Ade had lied to her about how his relationship with Cynthia had ended. If he could lie about that, maybe he was also lying about . . . Ife squeezes her eyes shut. She has to stop letting her thoughts go in that direction. Lying about one thing didn't make someone a killer. She's lying to him too, and, like her, he's probably just trying to protect her feelings.

'I'm sorry, okay.' His hand returns to her knee, and this time she is happy to let it rest there. 'It just feels like . . . like something isn't right. I mean, first the wedding, now this.'

'What do you mean . . . ?'

The fire alarm erupts around them. Ade is on his feet, and she follows him downstairs and into the kitchen, which is cloudy with smoke. He motions for her to stay back as he turns off the cooker, opens the windows and the back door to let the smoke out and the cold air in.

Once the kitchen has cleared, and his breakfast has been dumped in the bin, Ade leans against the counter, observes her for a moment, and then bursts out laughing.

It begins as a sob, and Ife thinks he's crying, instinctively moves closer to comfort him. But then his mouth widens, and his whole body shakes with laughter so he has to lean on her for support.

She rolls her eyes at him, though she is glad to see him laughing, even if it is at her cooking. 'I swear I turned it down.' This sends him into another fit of laughter.

When he is done, he pulls her into him and squeezes tight.

'I love you, Fey,' he tells her for the first time since before their wedding. 'You know that, right?' He looks into her eyes, and when she doesn't respond, he kisses her forehead and hugs her again.

'We should get going,' he says, pulling away from her. 'Time to meet our baby.'

CHAPTER NINETEEN

Three weeks before Cynthia's disappearance

'You look great, by the way,' Ife said when Cynthia returned from the bathroom. Cynthia had to admit that her skin was practically sparkling from the treatment that Ife had suggested. Even the aesthetician had been impressed by Ife's skincare knowledge, and, rather than feeling resentful, Cynthia had found herself handing over her phone so she could put in her product recommendations.

'Thanks.' Cynthia let Ife pour her another glass of Prosecco and downed it in one go. She smiled a smile that felt a little too big for her face, but she didn't care. She deserved to enjoy herself after what Ade had put her through, and, besides, Ife was smiling right back at her.

'So . . .' she said, linking arms with Ife as they made their way to the spa's café. 'You and Ade have *never* had a thing? Not even a little one?'

Ife paused, but Cynthia couldn't quite gauge her reaction.

'Well—' she began.

'I knew it!' The words escaped before Cynthia could stop them, and she winced, the bubbles drifting to her head.

Another painful pause as she waited for Ife to continue.

'I was speaking with Ade the other day,' she finally said. 'About what happened at dinner a couple of months back. I'm sorry I didn't say anything at the time. It was all just so—'

'No, it's fine,' Cynthia rushed in, noting that Ife's apology somehow seemed more sincere than Ade's had. 'I wouldn't mind so much if he actually had the balls to stand up to her.' She closed her eyes, once again regretting how quickly she'd spoken. Ife could easily relay all this to Ade, and then what?

'Yeah . . . neither can do wrong in the other's eyes. But I wouldn't worry about it. You're not the first girlfriend this has happened to.'

'Were you one of them?' Cynthia asked, returning to her initial question, not wanting to think about the deserted cemetery filled with relationships Mama had killed. 'You've known each other a long time. It seems almost inevitable that you would have—'

'Nope. Just friends.'

'Any reason?'

'Oh . . . he's not my type,' Ife said, gently unlinking her arm from Cynthia's and tucking her hands into the pockets of her hoodie. 'Besides, I know him too well . . . kind of ruins the magic, you know?'

'Yeah, makes sense.' Cynthia couldn't tell whether Ife

was uncomfortable because of the subject matter or because she was trying to hide the truth, and, in all honesty, she wasn't sure she *wanted* to know. Either way, it didn't matter. Not unless there was something going on between them now.

'So?' Cynthia put on her best Mama accent as they took their seats. 'Are you seeing anyone?'

Ife didn't even crack a smile.

'No, not for a while . . . I'd been in Dubai before Ade offered me a job, and now, well . . . I don't really have much time for romance.'

'Doesn't it get lonely?' Cynthia asked.

'It started to,' Ife admitted, studying the circular pattern on their table. 'That's why I came home.'

Cynthia had a sudden urge to give Ife a hug, but she wasn't *that* tipsy, so instead she changed the subject, asking Ife about her time in Dubai – and, later, for advice about Ade.

'Give him a chance to cool off,' she told her. 'He's more stubborn than usual when he's angry, but he'll come around.'

'Right.' Cynthia hadn't told Ife about Mark, and so her response didn't exactly fill her with optimism.

'Excuse me?'

They both swivelled their heads in the direction of the unexpected voice. It belonged to the man with dreadlocks Cynthia had seen hugging the receptionist earlier.

'Hi,' Cynthia smiled up at him, then glanced at Ife, whose eyes were practically glued to the carrot cake she was picking at with her fork.

'I think one of you ladies might have dropped this?'

He fished around his pocket and revealed a twenty-pence coin. Cynthia tried not to laugh at the cheesiness of the line and shook her head at him. He was laughing too, and the corners of his eyes creased into a smile that wasn't directed at her but at Ife, whose attention he had finally managed to grasp.

'Mind if I join you guys?' he asked, once his window was firmly established. 'This place is pretty packed.' Cynthia didn't need to look around to know that there were at least two empty tables he could sit at.

'You sure your girlfriend won't mind?' Cynthia asked, and he reluctantly turned his attention back to her.

'Sorry?'

'Tall, blonde, chews too much gum . . .' Cynthia replied, waving her hand in the general direction of the main reception area. The man's handsome face collapsed into one of genuine annoyance, he scrunched his face, and three almost imperceptible lines appeared on his forehead. 'That's my cousin. Her parents own this place,' he said. 'And yeah' – he cracked another Colgate smile at Ife – 'she does chew a lot of gum.'

'Right,' Cynthia nodded, and gestured at the seat next to Ife, giving him permission to sit down.

When he did, he offered his palm to Ife, and Ife placed her hand in his, smiling shyly.

'I'm Anton,' he said, wrapping his long, manicured fingers around her equally long, equally manicured ones.

'Ife,' she said.

'What a lovely name. Where's it from?'

'Um . . . Nigeria?' It sounded more like a question than a statement, but Anton, or Casanova, as Cynthia was now calling him in her head, soldiered on.

'Nigeria, huh? I've always wanted to go there.'

Cynthia downed the rest of her tiny cup of herbal tea, taking the brewing romance as her cue to pay and leave. She managed to catch Ife's eye and tilted her head towards the cashier to signal that she was leaving. Ife nodded and waved Cynthia goodbye before returning to her conversation with Anton, giggling as he whispered in her ear.

Cynthia made her way to the till and waited for the woman in front of her to finish paying. She told the cashier her table number, took her purse from her bag and opened it to get her bank card, only to discover that it was missing. At first, she thought someone had stolen it while she was getting her treatment, but she couldn't remember leaving it unattended. Besides, why would they only steal her card and not the whole purse?

'Excuse me, ma'am,' the cashier said.

'One sec.'

Cynthia opened the coin compartment and found the twenty-pound note she kept there, confirming that it probably wasn't a thief. Which only left one person pissed off enough to mess with her.

Once she'd paid for the drinks and Ife's carrot cake, she pulled out her phone to call him, but after two rings it went to voicemail. She tried again, and the same thing happened.

On her third try, it didn't even ring. She glanced over at Ife, but she was engrossed in her conversation with Anton, and Cynthia didn't want to disturb her.

Ade was meant to be picking her up, but she had no intention of waiting for him. She'd book a cab and confront him when she got home.

As she made her way through the grounds, Cynthia spotted a familiar car, parked in a corner a few metres from the front entrance. She wouldn't have noticed it if she hadn't been scanning the car park for Ade's Jag, just in case he'd turned up early.

Cynthia rapped on the window, and Mark almost flew through the roof when he saw her. Then he smiled and rolled down the window.

'Hey, what's up?' he said.

'Oh, nothing,' Cynthia replied, trying to figure out how to segue into why she needed a lift home. 'What are you doing here?'

Mark scratched his messy head. 'What? A man can't get a pedicure?'

'Really? You don't strike me as a pedicure kind of guy.'

'Looks can be deceiving.'

He seemed annoyed, and she immediately felt bad. Maybe he was waiting for his secret lady friend.

'Sorry,' she said. 'I didn't mean to . . . I'll just . . .'

She turned to leave, but Mark grabbed her arm through the open window.

'No, it's fine. You just caught me off guard.' He studied her for a moment. 'Is everything okay?'

'Yes.' She sighed. 'No, not really. I need to get home, but—'

'I'll take you.'

'No,' she shook her head. 'It's fine—'

'Cynthia.' He unlocked the door. 'Let me take you home.'

Mark obviously hadn't meant it that way, but she suddenly felt warm.

'Okay,' she croaked, rushing to the other side of the car in embarrassment.

She got in, and the car roared to life.

'Tell me everything,' Mark said.

CHAPTER TWENTY

Ife, present day

At the hospital, Ade is silent. As Ife lies on the bed waiting for the doctor to arrive, she wonders if he's thinking about the ring, about his breakup with Cynthia, about whether or not he wants to be with her. She considers telling him that Mark had given her the ring, but what good would that do? It wouldn't explain how the ring found its way into the house, and if what Mark said about Ade being jealous of him and Cynthia was true, it would only make him angry to know that he'd approached Ife.

The doctor, a short stubby man with a smooth bald head, enters the room with a nurse, who is tall and pale, with a head full of curly auburn hair trying to escape from her ponytail.

The doctor introduces himself and explains the procedure. His voice is soft and patient, soothing.

Ade, on the other hand, is anything but relaxed. He's taken her hand, the one that a few moments earlier Ife had been swinging from the side of the bed to prevent herself from biting her nails, and is gripping it tightly. Still, Ife can't bring herself to look at him.

The doctor asks her to lift her top and tells her that the gel they are going to apply will be cold. She braces herself, but the cool gooey substance is strangely comforting.

The doctor takes the ultrasound device, places it on Ife's belly, and moves it around. She waits, suspended in time, for the sound she thinks she's supposed to hear. She's watched enough soaps, she thinks, to know what should be happening. He moves the device around more, his brow furrowed with concentration, and Ife wonders what's going on.

Perhaps there is nothing there. Perhaps she's made this whole thing up, has wished herself pregnant so badly that she has somehow managed to manifest real symptoms.

There is no baby, she says to herself, and squeezes Ade's hand. Everyone's going to think I'm a liar. He's going to leave me.

'Ah, there we go,' the doctor says, and he's back to smiling again. 'Hear that?' he asks, then points towards a small screen. 'The baby's heart.'

Tears spring to Ife's eyes as she looks at the little human that lives inside her and listens to the rhythm of its heartbeat. She is relieved that the baby exists, that it is not a figment of her imagination, that she has not simply convinced her body to do the one thing she needs to keep her family together.

The relief is followed by amazement at the fact that she's quite literally growing another person. It seems more real than it ever has, yet somehow strange that this baby, that did not exist before, is now suddenly something with a heartbeat; that her body, for the next few months, is going to be its home, and that for the rest of her life she will be responsible for its well-being. Her and no one else.

She looks up at Ade, who now seems far away. He's looking at the screen, but his eyes seem vacant, like he is here in his body but his mind has wandered somewhere else altogether.

Her responsibility, she thinks again. And hers alone.

The drive home is just as quiet as the one they'd made there. Ade stares straight ahead and doesn't even turn on his music. Although he's quiet, he also seems calm, his lips settled in a wistful smile.

'Need anything from the shops?' Ade asks as they approach the roundabout that leads to the only Tesco in the area.

'No, I'm fine.' Ife keeps her eyes on the road.

'What, not even pickles and peanut butter?'

Ife remains silent, remembering the jar of pickles she'd polished off the night before.

He turns into the supermarket anyway and parks.

'That was amazing, wasn't it?' he says, switching off the engine.

'It was,' Ife says, finally allowing herself to smile.

'The way he just popped up on the screen like that. And his heartbeat! I didn't think it would sound like that.'

'His?' Ife asks. 'You think it's a boy?'

'Of course,' Ade laughs. 'Couldn't you tell? He looks just like me.'

'Yes, Ade, he clearly had your eyes.' Ife rolls her own eyes at him. 'Does it matter? If it's a boy or a girl, I mean?'

He has to think about this. His eyebrows furrow as he hugs the steering wheel.

'No. No, not really,' he replies after a few moments. 'Although, knowing Mum, she'll probably want a grandson straight away. She always used to say that *my first grandchild must be a boy oh.* I never really understood that. She's spent most of her adult life taking care of two unruly boys. Why would she want a grandson?'

Ife swallows. It's a conversation she's had with Mama too.

'My mum was the same,' she says, not wanting to remember her run-ins with Mama. 'The last time I saw her, she was getting really excited about it for some reason. I didn't even have a boyfriend.'

'It must be tough,' Ade says, placing a hand over hers. 'Not having your mum here.' Ade had met her mother on a few occasions when she'd come to visit from Nigeria. At the time, Ade had told her that he was amazed at how different she was from his own mother and her friends, who were loud and liked to gossip. *I thought all Nigerian women were like that*, he'd said, and Ife had rolled her eyes at him.

Now Ife doesn't respond, and he continues to speak, his voice tentative, as if he isn't sure how she'll react to what he's going to say next.

'Listen, Fey.' His hand is still on hers, and he shifts in his seat so he's facing her. 'I know I've been a bit off lately. This whole Cynthia thing . . . it's like she's in my head *all the fucking time*.' He looks like he's about to cry, but Ife doesn't move.

'I promise I'm going to do better,' he continues. 'For the baby, I have to do better. For us too,' he adds, and Ife thinks this is an afterthought. 'I want this marriage to work.'

She wants to believe him, wants their marriage to work too, but there are so many lies between them now, so much doubt about the future.

'Ade,' she says. 'The night that Cynthia disappeared . . . do you know where she might have gone?' She wants him to admit that he knew she'd been living with Mark, that she'd moved on and he was fine with it. Instead, he shakes his head.

'I don't know,' he says. 'I don't know.'

'Maybe if we tried to find out—'

'No,' Ade snaps. 'I don't want you getting involved in this, Ife. Let the police do their job.'

'Okay.' Ife fiddles with her seat belt.

'Good,' he says. 'Now, let's go get your pickles and peanut butter.'

By the time they arrive back at the house, the ice between them seems to have thawed, and Ife allows herself to picture what their lives will be like when the baby arrives. Ade making late-night nappy runs. Ade's hand around her shoulder as she pushes the baby's pram. Ade rocking the baby to sleep every single night as she watches from their bed.

Present Ade eases the car into the driveway. There's a police car parked outside, and Ade swears under his breath.

'What do they want now?' he mutters, as the police officer slams her car door shut and makes her way towards them.

Except she doesn't go over to Ade's side of the car as Ife expects her to. Instead, she stops by the passenger door, leaving little room for escape.

'Mrs Dolapo,' the officer says. 'Can I have a word?'

CHAPTER TWENTY-ONE

Three weeks before Cynthia's disappearance

Someone was singing in the kitchen.

Cynthia shut the front door gently behind her, and listened as Mama belted out words in a language she couldn't understand. For a moment, she was distracted from her anger, Mama's soulful voice eliciting a sense of sadness she didn't know she was feeling. She closed her eyes and rested her head against the door, letting the sadness wash over her, wishing that it hadn't come to this.

But Mark had been right last night when he'd said Ade needed to trust her, and he'd been right on the drive home when he'd told her she'd be a fool if she stayed.

Nothing was ever that simple though, and, as hurt as she was, she figured Ade at least deserved a chance to explain. Maybe it was a coincidence that Ife had shown up at the spa, or that her card was missing, just like it was a coincidence that she'd run into Mark.

'Adebayo, is that you?' Mama called from the kitchen.

Ade wasn't even home, and now she was stuck in the house with a woman who hated her and wanted her gone. Yet another reason to listen to Mark's advice.

Then again, what did Mark know? He had a failed marriage, an ex-wife who couldn't stand him and a secret crush he'd apparently upended his entire life for. He wasn't exactly a shining example of healthy relationships.

'Oh, it's you.' Cynthia could hear the disappointment in Mama's voice before she opened her eyes to see it etched into the purse of her lips. She was holding a large kitchen knife, her hands fatty with meat. 'Come and help me in the kitchen,' she said.

'I, uh . . .' Cynthia began, pointing in the opposite direction of where Mama wanted her to go. But Mama was having none of it, and she looked Cynthia up and down before turning on her heels, leaving her with no choice but to follow.

'Where's Ade?' Cynthia asked, taking in the bowl of meat sitting next to the chopping board and the large cast-iron pot that didn't belong to Cynthia.

'Pass me that small knife over there.' Mama gestured with her butcher's knife to the counter behind Cynthia. 'He is out with his brother. I wanted to come home and cook so he gave me the key.'

Great. There was no telling how long they were going to be.

'Well,' Mama said, reaching behind Cynthia for the knife she'd failed to retrieve and then flashing Cynthia a deceptively sunny smile. 'How did your spa-ing go?'

Like her son, Mama knew how to turn on the fake charm when she wanted to, but Cynthia wasn't about to stand there and pretend that she hadn't heard exactly what she'd said the night before.

'Actually, I'm pretty tired,' she said, rubbing her eyes to emphasise her point. It was a flimsy excuse, but Cynthia was far beyond caring. This was her house, and she could do whatever the hell she wanted. 'I'm going to lie down.'

'Ah ah.' Mama kissed her teeth. 'Did you not just spend the whole day lying down?' She grabbed a brown paper bag and spread its contents onto another chopping board. 'Come and chop this okra for me.'

Cynthia eyed the long green stems and frowned. As a child, she'd always thought they looked like alien fingers and would cry every time she was commanded to chop them, their slimy, extraterrestrial interior covering her hands.

'Come on,' Mama said, holding the knife out to her. 'Or do your people not eat okra?'

Cynthia dug her nails into the palms of her hands to keep herself from saying something sassy back. Despite the numerous hours she'd spent in the shower dreaming up cutting comebacks to Mama's comments, Cynthia could never actually use any of them. Maybe it was the way she was raised to never talk back to her elders no matter how insolent they were being. She was too polite for her own damn good.

Instead, Cynthia grumbled under her breath as she washed her hands and began chopping the okra, wincing after every first slice. Mama returned to her own chopping and began to sing again. Her voice filled the room, negating the need for conversation, and the pair of them stayed like this – side by side – until Mama plopped her last piece of meat into the pot.

Once she'd scrubbed her hands clean, Mama pulled a bottle of peach schnapps and two larger-than-average shot glasses from one of her Ghana Must Go bags.

She poured and handed one to Cynthia, her tight-lipped expression daring her to refuse. Cynthia took it, they both downed their drinks, and Mama poured another for the two of them. Cynthia raised an eyebrow, wondering whether Mama was trying to get her drunk and to what end. She could probably outdrink Mama if she wanted to, but she was still feeling a little tipsy from the Prosecco, and she needed to keep her wits about her.

Mama drank her drink, placed her glass on the table and waited for Cynthia to do the same. Cynthia sighed and drank. Surprisingly, she liked the taste. It reminded her of her favourite pick 'n' mix and Saturday mornings browsing in Woolworths with her own mother.

She waited for Mama to pour again, but instead she screwed the lid back onto the bottle and returned to her pot of meat. Cynthia went back to chopping the okra.

'It needs to be finer,' Mama said without even looking at her chopping board, and Cynthia sighed. It felt like the pile of okra wasn't getting any smaller, a feeling aggravated by the fact that her head was beginning to feel light. She had to take her time now to make sure she didn't cut her fingers off instead.

'So,' Mama said. She was adding onions and seasoning to the meat and shaking the pot so the small flaps of her arms jiggled. 'You want to marry my son.'

'And I can't even say efo properly.' Cynthia let out an unladylike snort and covered her mouth, spreading tiny okra seeds all over her face.

Mama frowned at her. 'What are you talking about?'

'That green thing you made. With spinach? Tasted good . . .'

'Efo.'

'Say it again.' Mama did, slowly this time.

'Again.'

Mama kissed her teeth. 'You are a very foolish girl.'

Cynthia shrugged and returned her attention to the chopping board. Tipsy tears stung her eyes. Mama was right: she was foolish. Foolish for thinking Mama might one day accept her. That Ade would choose her. That he even cared. This entire day had proved that they were no longer on the same page. So maybe Mama would finally get what she wanted.

'You insult me.' Mama broke the silence. 'You really think that is why I don't want you to marry my son?'

Cynthia didn't bother looking up. 'Why then? Because I *shake my nyash* for a living?' She air quoted the last part, feeling clever for using Mama's words against her. She was surprised, then, when Mama nodded her head in agreement.

'You will make each other miserable,' she told her. 'He deserves to be with someone who will make him happy.'

Cynthia sniffed. 'We were fine, before . . .' – she waved her hands trying to find the right words; *before you came along and fucked everything up* probably wouldn't go over well – 'all this happened.'

'I know my son,' she insisted. 'He needs someone who needs him. Who is not as stubborn as him.'

'Someone like Ife, you mean?'

'She loves him. It is the kind of love that has stood the test of time.'

'But he doesn't love her.' She wanted to say *he loves me*, that she loved him, but Cynthia wasn't sure about either of those things anymore.

'He will.' Mama touched Cynthia's shoulder, and through her tears, she saw Mama handing her another shot. It went down more smoothly this time. 'Under the right circumstances, he will.'

Soon, Cynthia found herself sitting at the dining-room table opposite Mama who looked like a blurry blob.

There was still no sign of Tayo and Ade, but Cynthia didn't mind. Now that she knew the truth, she felt renewed somehow. She also had no intention of letting Mama win.

Except now there were two of her. Cynthia blinked several times, noticed that her purple-lipsticked mouth was moving, but all she could hear was incomprehensible mumbling.

'What?' Cynthia croaked. She felt so tired. Maybe she should just go to bed.

She stood up, stumbling as she tried to leave the table, but Mama was shaking her head.

'You need to eat' came out slowly, and Mama's voice was deeper than it usually was. Cynthia sat back down and squinted as Mama dished rice and okra and stew onto a plate. She handed her a fork and dug into her own dinner, crossing herself before taking a bite.

Cynthia mimicked the action, though she wasn't sure why. She took a bite. Mama was still talking, and, although she couldn't hear much of what she was saying, Cynthia could feel herself nodding enthusiastically and smiling.

Cynthia took another bite. And another. And . . . She coughed. Her skin began to tingle, her throat began to itch. She coughed again. It felt like someone had set fire to a colony of ants in her mouth, and she waved at Mama, trying to get her attention.

Mama looked at her and frowned.

'Are you okay?' Mama's lips said, but she didn't get up, didn't come to her rescue.

Somewhere in the distance, she thought she heard a door close, but she couldn't be sure because her chest was tight now, and it was getting harder and harder to breathe.

CHAPTER TWENTY-TWO

Ife, present day

'So, Mrs Dolapo,' the blonde police officer who had introduced herself as Detective Callaghan says, her demeanour far too calm for the circumstances. She takes a sip of the tea Ife has made for her, spilling some of it as she returns her cup to its saucer.

Ife, on the other hand, is anything but calm. Her legs are shaking furiously under the table, and she can only hope that Ade, who is sitting next to her, can't feel how panicked she is. She'd told him she could handle the police on her own, but he'd insisted on staying right by her side. If she hadn't been so worried about what the police were going to say, her heart would have soared.

'What was your relationship with the deceased?'

'I . . . we didn't have one,' Ife stammers and then winces at her own nervousness. 'I didn't really know her,' she adds firmly.

'So, the two of you never met?'

'I didn't say that,' Ife says slowly, picking at her fingernails. 'We met maybe once or twice, but, like I said, I didn't know her all that well.'

'And you met her through your now husband, is that correct?'

Ife nods.

'When was the last time you saw her?'

'This is ridiculous.'

Ife breathes a silent sigh of relief at Ade's interruption. 'They met each other once, and barely even spoke. If you think harassing my pregnant wife will somehow bring you closer to the truth, you've got another thing coming. We . . .' – he covers her hand with his – 'had nothing to do with this.'

'You're pregnant?' Detective Callaghan's expression stiffens as she sits up in her seat, suddenly all business. 'How far, if you don't mind me asking?'

Ife can tell the detective is doing calculations in her head, putting two and two together to make five, and her answer sticks in her throat.

She's done nothing wrong – well, nothing *criminal*. If the police genuinely thought she had something to do with Cynthia's murder, she would be in handcuffs right now, not sipping tea at her kitchen table.

Still, if she answers this question, only God knows where it might lead. And even though it hadn't been her fault, not really, she is almost certain Ade won't see it that way.

'You don't have to answer that,' Ade comes to her rescue again, placing a gentle hand on her shaking knee.

At this, Detective Callaghan tucks her sharply cut blonde hair behind her ear, closes her folder and slips it into the black leather bag on her lap. 'If you don't want to talk now,' she says, 'then we can all have a more formal conversation tomorrow. At the station.'

Ife and Ade exchange a silent glance, and then Ife sighs.

'A few months,' she says. 'But it's not what you're thinking.'

'Oh?' Detective Callaghan returns her folder to the table. 'And what am I thinking?'

'That we had an affair. That Ade got me pregnant and didn't want Cynthia to find out. That we . . .' She hesitates, unable to say the words out loud. 'But that's not what happened. Ade didn't even know until a couple of days ago.'

'Is that true, Mr Dolapo?'

Ade sits back in his seat, momentarily triumphant. 'I'm many things, detective,' he says. 'But I'm not a cheater.'

Detective Callaghan observes him for a few seconds, but says nothing. Instead, she clicks her pen, up and down, up and down, up and down, the sound like a ticking clock, counting down to her next accusation. Ife feels an almost uncontrollable urge to flee, and she tenses the muscles in her legs to keep them from carrying her away.

The clicking stops.

The kitchen falls silent.

Ife waits for Detective Callaghan to speak, but instead she takes another sip of her tea.

CHAPTER TWENTY-THREE

Three weeks before Cynthia's disappearance

Cynthia could feel her tongue swelling in her mouth, her airway rapidly closing off as she fought for air. She thumped her fists against the table, hoping that it would wake Mama from whatever trance she was in.

She was in shock. That was the only reason Mama was still sitting right across from her, arms crossed, lips pursed, as if Cynthia had just told her a dirty joke. That was the only reason she wasn't doing everything in her power to save her.

The room was spinning now, and Cynthia grappled for Mama's hand as the world slowly slipped from her grasp. She saw Ade, her love, smiling down at her. Mark, her friend, telling her she'd be okay. Tayo announcing that he was home.

Suddenly Mama was on her feet, patting her back, asking her if she needed water.

Another voice, Ade's, called her name in a panic.

'What did you do?' he shouted.

'Me ke? She was choking. I was trying to help her.'

The room fell silent, and for one long moment she was sure that it was over. Thought it wasn't so bad, being dead.

But then she felt a warm, soft hand in hers, and she squinted to see Tayo's troubled expression.

'Hold on, C,' he said. 'Please just hold on.'

His hand fell away, and Cynthia felt a prick in her thigh.

Her body flooded with relief and then panic as her heart rate escalated.

Ade was hugging her. 'Thank God,' he said. 'Thank God.'

And then he turned to Mama.

'Adebayo . . .' she began.

'Get out,' he said softly.

'Please now.' Mama dropped to her knees, wringing her hands. 'I don't know what happened . . . she just started . . .'

Ade left the room before she could finish, and Tayo took Cynthia's hand again.

'Are you okay?' he asked, and she nodded. Her breathing was gradually returning to normal, but she couldn't speak, not when Hurricane Ade was storming back into the room with one of Mama's Ghana Must Go bags in tow. He dropped an empty plastic packet on the table.

'Did you put this in her food?'

Mama rose to her feet and stared at the packet. Cynthia squinted through the headache that was forming but couldn't quite make out what it said.

'Crayfish,' Tayo whispered.

'I . . . Adebayo, please,' Mama said. 'I didn't know.'

'I told you . . .' Ade took a breath. For a moment, Cynthia thought he was going to walk away, to let it be, but then he hurled the rice and plates and cutlery off the table in one quick swoop, sending them crashing to floor at Mama's feet. He took Mama by the arm and tried to push her towards the door, but she refused to budge.

'I want her gone.' He jabbed a finger in Tayo's face before picking up the Ghana Must Go bag and charging up the stairs.

'Mum, just go,' Tayo told her.

'Will you shut up your mouth,' she snapped. 'Oya, Cynthia. Go and talk to your husband. Tell him how I was helping you.'

Husband? Helping her? Was she mad? Cynthia kept her eyes glued on the shattered plates, refusing to even look at Mama. After what she'd tried to do, did she really expect Cynthia to defend her? She tried to stand up so she could leave, but she was stopped by the fact that her head was spinning and by the sound of Ade's angry footsteps. There was a loud crash in the driveway and then Ade was back.

'You're still here,' Ade muttered before lifting Mama off the ground and carrying her out of the room.

'Ah ah. Adebayo,' Cynthia heard Mama say before the front door slammed shut.

'Babe.' Ade returned to the room and knelt next to her,

taking her hands in his. There was so much remorse in that single word that Cynthia almost squeezed his hand to comfort him.

But it was too late, and she was too angry. It was the kind of anger that came with having one's fears realised.

She stumbled up to their bedroom and slammed the door, hating the fact that their relationship had come full circle and she was once again packing her bags because of Mama. This time Ade did everything he could to stop her, but it was Cynthia's turn to keep silent as he followed her around the house and begged her not to leave, saying all the things she'd waited months for him to say, Tayo behind him, telling him to *just leave it man* and *give her space*. Eventually, Ade shoved Tayo into a wall and told him to back the hell off.

The entire time Cynthia was on autopilot, drifting from room to room, collecting random items she knew she didn't need: a Russian doll, a container of cotton buds, a mushy frame that reminded them to *live, laugh, love.*

All the while her mind was racing to figure out what to do next. She needed to get to the hospital, but she knew Ade would insist on going with her when all she wanted to do was get away from him. She had nowhere else to go, no one else to help her.

Except Mark.

She didn't want to bother him, but what choice did she

have now? She'd go to the studio as soon as she had all her things, would pay part of the rent for as long as she stayed with him, even though she was sure he would refuse it. And then she remembered.

'What happened to my card?' Cynthia swung on Ade, who was so rattled he nearly fell down the stairs.

'What do you mean?'

'I couldn't pay for my tea today because I couldn't find my card. What did you do with it?'

'Nothing, I swear. Maybe you . . .'

Cynthia glared at him, silently daring him to finish his sentence.

'I'll help you look for it,' he said instead. 'Just wait here, okay.' He dashed down the stairs, and Cynthia went into their bedroom to pack some of her clothes before leaving Ade with his hands down the sofa and driving the short distance to the studio.

She lugged her belongings up the stairs to Mark's apartment and knocked, trying to decide what to tell him.

As soon as he opened the door, dressed only in a pair of stripy boxers, he swore under his breath. Cynthia looked down at the dark blotches on her arm, which were probably all over her face too. She'd been so focused on packing her bags that she'd lost sight of the reason she was leaving in the first place. But as her watery eyes took in Mark's horrified expression, she realised she needed medical attention. Now.

Mark must have read her mind because he motioned for her phone, which she held in her shaking hand. She passed it over and she watched, frozen, as he dialled for an ambulance and carried her bags inside, probably expecting her to follow. She listened to his muffled voice as he spoke to the operator, unable to move, her fingernails digging into the palms of her hands.

'Cynthia,' she heard him say, and she could picture him turning around, his surprised expression as he discovered she wasn't there. He was back outside in a flash.

'Hey,' he said, holding his hand out for hers.

Cynthia sobbed, a deep, heavy sob that emerged from the pit of her stomach, leaving her doubled over, breathless.

And just like that, she broke. Right there on his doorstep, covered in hives and grief, she fell into Mark's arms, her hot relentless tears soaking his bare shoulder as he held her.

CHAPTER TWENTY-FOUR

Ife, present day

Detective Callaghan's steel-blue eyes focus in on Ife, and Ife forces herself not to blink. In the corner of her eye, she sees, or thinks she sees, a shadow rushing past the kitchen door. Her entire body goes rigid. Sweat pools in her bra.

Finally, the detective speaks.

'Let me make sure I'm understanding this correctly,' she says to Ade. Her voice is calm, measured, but beneath that Ife notes a touch of disbelief. 'You and Miss Bennet break up in early August – amicably, according to the statement you gave us. Correct?'

Ade nods.

'Almost immediately, you take up with the now *Mrs* Dolapo, who, by your own admission, was well aware that you and Miss Bennet had been in a committed relationship. Also correct?'

'It wasn't exactly immediate,' Ade mumbles, a lie Ife finds no reason to correct.

'And somewhere between your breakup with Miss Bennet and you and Mrs Dolapo . . .' She pauses, waving her hand in search of the appropriate phrase.

'Hooking up?' Ade offers.

His words sting. She knows he doesn't mean them, knows he's being snarky because he's agitated, but she can't help but wonder if deep down his words hold some truth.

'Between your breakup and *that*,' the detective continues, 'Miss Bennet disappears off the face of the earth, only to be found washed up on the shore a few months later. But neither of you had anything to do with it, because you, Mr Dolapo, were absolutely fine about the unexpected conclusion of what you called a serious relationship, and you, Mrs Dolapo, had absolutely no interest in Mr Dolapo up until that point. Correct?'

Neither of them respond. Put like that, Ife can see why they look guilty. The timing of their marriage, the fact that it coincided with Cynthia's body turning up. It all makes it seem like they were involved. But, as much as Ife hates to admit it, this is a dance that she and Ade have been doing for decades.

She'd thought the dance had ended in her second year at Surrey when he'd shown up at her accommodation unannounced. She'd been planning to meet her boyfriend, Kwame, after she dropped her books in her room, when she'd found Ade sitting outside her door, playing with his phone.

Her heart betrayed her by doing its mandatory backflip, and Ife forced herself not to react when he flashed his bone-melting smile and wrapped her in a bear hug, lifting her off the ground. Remaining stoic, she asked him what he was doing there.

'Do I need an excuse to come and see my bestie?'

'No,' Ife said, ignoring the flutter in her tummy. 'But a warning would have been nice.'

'Since when?'

'Why aren't you at uni?'

'Since when?'

Ife unlocked her door and shoved it open. She already knew why he was there, even if he was too much of a coward to admit it. Just like she was too much of a coward to call him out on it.

'Since I don't want people showing up at my place unannounced.'

'Rah, so I'm people now?'

No, he could never be people to her, but she wasn't about to tell him that.

Ife had dropped her books on her desk and slid lip gloss, the one Kwame said he liked, across her lips. All the while, she remained silent, until Ade finally revealed that he'd just broken up with his latest girlfriend, Jennifer. If you could call Ade's three-month overblown flings relationships.

This hadn't come as a surprise. Of course he was only there because he was between women. Still, she reasoned, he'd travelled all the way from Oxford to see her, and didn't that mean something?

No. Because she had a guy who really liked her waiting to take her out, and she wasn't going to ruin it because of Ade. Not again.

'Look, I've got to go,' she told him.

'Lecture?'

'No.'

'Can I come?'

'No.' She took a deep breath. 'I have a date with Kwame.'

'Who?'

Ife glared at him.

'Can't you cancel? I really need you right now.'

Ife turned to find him sitting on her bed, lips pursed like a child whose favourite toy had just been confiscated. She didn't have time for this. Kwame was probably wondering where she was, imagining all kinds of things.

'Fey . . .'

'What?'

Ade sighed. 'Forget it.'

'Okay,' Ife said, doing the exact opposite of what he expected. 'I'll be back in a couple of hours. Don't touch my stuff.'

Later that evening, Ife had returned to halls to find Ade in the kitchen. Coffee with Kwame had been awkward, and she'd gone shopping afterwards in the hope that Ade would eventually grow bored of waiting for her and leave.

'You're still here?' she'd said, making a face at him.

'Why you acting like that for?'

'Like what?'

'Like you're not damn well pleased to see me.'

The ego! 'I'm not.'

'Woow, so it's like that, yeah?'

Ife shrugged.

'Okay.' Ade blew out a sigh. 'I'm sorry for showing up unannounced. I'll call you next time.'

'Text.'

Ade frowned at her, eyebrows furrowed in confusion, then sighed again.

'You hungry?' he asked. 'I made spaghetti.'

Ife looked inside one of the pots. Bolognese.

'Since when did you know how to cook?'

'Since Jennifer taught me.'

'So you two were serious?'

He had the audacity to look hurt. 'All my relationships are serious,' he'd said.

They'd eaten in her room watching reruns of *My Wife and Kids* on her laptop.

Between episodes, Ade asked her how her date went. His tone seemed condescending, as if he couldn't possibly imagine Ife having a date, let alone a good one.

'None of your business,' she'd snapped.

Ade smacked his fork against his empty plate.

'What the hell is wrong with you today?'

Ife ignored him, took another bite of her annoyingly delicious spaghetti and returned her attention to the screen. Ade grabbed her laptop and slammed it shut.

'Why would you do that?' Ife said, trying and failing to retrieve her laptop.

'Tell me what's wrong.'

'Nothing.'

'Bullshit.'

They'd glared at each other, neither of them willing to look away. Ife thought she felt something sizzle between them, but then didn't she always think she felt that? And wasn't it always her imagination?

'Tell me,' he repeated.

'It's just . . .'

'Go on . . .'

Ife gave him the side-eye, and he held his hands up in surrender.

'Why are you here?'

He shrugged. 'I wanted to see you. Why is that so bad?'

Ife hated where this conversation was going, hated that she had to spell it out for him. She wrestled his plate from his hands and marched into the kitchen, hoping to leave their conversation behind her.

She dumped the dishes into the sink and turned on the

hot water, allowing it to run over the back of her hand, letting the heat distract her from the pain in her chest.

He knew how she felt about him, and yet all he cared about was making himself feel better. He didn't want to be alone, so he had to come and ruin what was supposed to be a romantic afternoon with Kwame. Him being here complicated everything. Why couldn't he see that?

Ife snatched her hand away from the steaming water and blew on it several times to soothe the stinging.

'Let me see.'

She hadn't heard him coming up behind her, and now he was so close she could feel his breath tickling her neck, his tall frame lumbering over her. Protective. Suffocating.

Ignoring the tears stinging her eyes, Ife squeezed the last of the washing-up liquid onto each of the plates.

'I'll do it,' he said softly.

She shook her head, and two droplets of salty water fell into the sink.

'Are you crying?'

Ife rubbed the sponge across one of the plates then turned it over so she could clean the other side.

'Ife, look at me.'

She raised her eyes to the heavens and wiped her tears with her sleeve. Then she turned to face him.

His face crumpled. She tried to push past him, but he blocked her path.

'I'm sorry,' he said, as if that would solve anything. 'I know things have been different with us since . . . that things need to change, but . . .' He paused. 'Do you know why Jennifer broke up with me?'

Ife sniffed and shook her head. He raised an eyebrow, tilted his head, and smiled.

Oh.

'Yeah, I couldn't shut up about you.'

'But you said . . .' She didn't believe him, but she desperately wanted to.

'I know,' he interrupted. 'But sometimes I wonder if maybe I was wrong. God knows you're the only girl . . . woman . . . who actually gets me.'

'Which is why things need to change.'

He nodded. 'Honestly, Fey, I'm just as confused as you are. I don't know how I feel . . . only that I can't stand that look you're giving me right now. I mean, do you hate me?'

She shook her head.

'Come here then.'

She'd stepped into his arms. They were so close she could feel his heart beating, and even in her disbelief she knew where this was going, had dreamt it a million and one times.

But they couldn't do this. Not here in the kitchen, where anyone could see. Not now, when she was unavailable.

She tried to shift away from him, really she did, but he

wrapped his arms more tightly around her and somehow managed to pull her even closer.

'I don't want to lose you,' he murmured against her ear.

She looked up into his eyes, filled with the desperation of his words, and she could see that maybe, just maybe, he meant them.

Keeping his eyes on hers, he tucked her straightened hair behind her ear, and then, in one swift move, his lips were on hers, gentle at first, tentative. Dipping his toe in the water to see how cold it was.

Ife's lips tingled from his touch, and he kissed her again, more urgently this time.

It never felt like this with Kwame. Sultry. Electrifying.

And even though she knew it was wrong, knew they needed to stop, her heart had different ideas.

Moments later she was pressed against the kitchen cabinet, Ade kissing her neck as he slipped his hands under her skirt.

Babes, what the hell are you doing? she heard Demi say, but Ife couldn't bear to listen. Even now, Demi still didn't understand how much she needed him. And so she pressed on, dipped her head and kissed him again. He sighed, hoisted her onto the countertop and stepped between her legs.

I thought you were better than this, Ife. Or have you already forgotten what I told you?

This time Demi's words hit home. Ife's eyes snapped open, and the kitchen shifted into focus. Lust burned into uncontainable rage, and she pushed him. Hard.

Ade's own eyes flew open.

'What the . . . ?'

She'd pushed him again and again and again, all the love and hurt and confusion she'd kept bottled up for far too long finally pouring out, only slowing when Ade grabbed hold of both of her hands.

'Fey?' She stopped struggling against him, her body deflating like an overused basketball. His expression was frozen in shock, eyes wide, mouth slightly agape.

'I don't care if you're mad at me,' she told him. It was a lie. She cared far too much, but she also hated what he'd just made her do.

'I'm not mad,' he said. His voice was warm, soothing. 'I'm just worried about you, Fey.'

'Then why do you keep doing this to me?'

'What do you mean?' He sounded so very confused. 'I thought this was what you wanted.'

He almost had her there, but then Kwame's shy smile flashed in her mind and she was filled with a sickening shame.

'Just leave me alone,' she'd told him, breaking free from his grip.

She'd rushed to her room, chucked his backpack outside and locked the door.

Instead of leaving, he had spent what felt like for ever banging on her door, demanding she let him in, asking her if she was okay. He only stopped when one of her housemates, Ian, came to her rescue.

'Probably best to leave it, mate,' he'd told him, and the banging had stopped.

When Ife awoke at around 2 a.m., her eyes were sore, her mouth was dry, and she had a throbbing headache. She squinted at the bright light on her phone. There was a message from Kwame.

Night beautiful, it said. Hope you were able to sort things with your friend. Hate seeing you sad xxx

Ife swallowed. Her throat felt like someone had tried to sand it down with a nail file. She was going to have to break up with him, and only now, in the stark light of her shame, did she realise how much he'd come to mean to her. And now, because she'd been so caught up in her feelings for Ade, she'd lost them both.

Except when Ife had left for her lecture later that morning, Ade was sleeping against the wall outside her room. She managed to slip past him unnoticed, but later that night he'd sent her a two-page text message apologising for hurting her but not for kissing her.

It's the most honest thing I've ever done, he said. *I love you, Fey. Please, just talk to me.*

Her feelings stirred, of course they did, but she ignored

them, and him. Even if he didn't realise it, he was just biding his time until his next fling, using her to ease his loneliness.

For a full year, she didn't speak to him, didn't text him, only checked his Facebook every other day.

Eventually, he'd stopped trying to contact her, and Ife had thought that their friendship was officially over, until he'd shown up with her aunt at her graduation with a bouquet of flowers and a bottle of the perfume she no longer wore because it reminded her too much of him.

They'd become friends again, leaving that night in the kitchen as an unspoken memory. They met up regularly for coffee or dinner but always avoided the topic of romantic partners. And then, a few months after she moved to Dubai, he just stopped responding, deactivated his Facebook, and she never heard from him again.

Of course, she'd been devastated, but it wasn't until she lost her job and her mum all in the same year that the loneliness really hit her. She'd moved back to England to stay with her aunt and get back on her feet. It was there, when Mama came to pay her respects, that she'd invited Ife to dinner.

She hadn't known about Cynthia, hadn't known what Mama was plotting. The way she'd made it sound, Ade knew she was coming and couldn't wait to see her. By the time Ife realised that it was all a ruse to break Ade and

Cynthia up, it was too late. She had already become Mama's puppet.

Now, she realises, they might have unknowingly fallen back into old patterns. But that doesn't mean that what Detective Callaghan is implying is correct. Sure, maybe Ade had been uncharacteristically upset when he'd shown up at her house that night in August, but it was one thing for him to seek her out after a breakup, and an entirely different thing to use her to cover up a murder.

As much as he's hurt her over the years, she knows he wouldn't do that to her, or to Cynthia for that matter.

'Maybe everything you said is true,' Ade says, squeezing her knee. 'But the only crime I've committed is taking too long to realise that Fey is the person I've always needed. If that makes me look like a murderer then so be it.'

A wave of guilt washes over her at the fact that she'd doubted his feelings for her when all he's been trying to do is protect her. 'If that's everything, detective . . .' Ife rises to her feet, hoping to end the interrogation there.

'It's not.' Detective Callaghan motions for Ife to sit, and Ife acquiesces, crossing her legs tightly together. 'Can you tell me where you were on 25 July?'

'I . . . I'm not sure.'

Detective Callaghan pulls a sheet of paper from her folder. 'Maybe this will jog your memory,' she says, sliding it over to her. 'Do you recognise this place?'

Ade is leaning forward, trying to get a closer look, and Ife wishes she could grab the CCTV image of her and Cynthia at Wild Cherry Spa, scrunch it up and chuck it in the bin.

Instead, she nods.

'You said you hardly knew each other, and yet there the two of you are,' she says. 'Looking like the best of friends.'

Ife shifts in her seat, not daring to look at Ade, who has suddenly gone very still beside her.

'I . . . uh . . .' Ife stutters.

'I set it up,' Ade says, coming to her rescue for a third time. 'I wanted the two women I cared most about in the world to get to know each other, so I booked them a spa day. Is that a crime too, detective?'

'I see,' Detective Callaghan says, not taking Ade's bait. 'And did she seem distressed in any way? Worried about something at home?' Ife shakes her head.

'Not really . . . she seemed pretty relaxed. We both got facials, a massage, had coffee and then went home. All in all, it was a nice day.'

'And did you see or speak to her again after that?'

'No, that was the last time I heard from her.' Ife stands to her feet. 'Now, if you'll excuse me, detective . . .'

This time, Detective Callaghan closes her folder and nods. Ife rushes to the downstairs toilet, and, as she sits there, she thinks about what she's going to say to Ade. Even though he'd defended her, he was bound to have questions, but she was afraid of how he would react to the answers. Maybe it would be better if she came clean, consequences be damned. Besides, there was clearly more to his breakup with Cynthia than what he'd told her. If she told the truth, maybe he would open up too.

Resolved, Ife flushes the toilet and goes to wash her hands.

There, sparkling in a pool of water, is Cynthia's ring.

Ife doesn't even try to convince herself that Ade has left it there by mistake. She stares at it, wondering if they're both going crazy, or if something more sinister is happening. She decides she doesn't care, that she has more pressing things to worry about. If she's losing her mind, or is on the receiving end of a curse, then so be it.

Taking a deep breath, she swipes the ring into the sink and down the drain then heads back to the kitchen where Ade is waiting for her, the detective long gone.

'I'm so sorry,' she begins. 'It was Mama's idea, and I foolishly went along with it.'

'It's fine,' he says. 'I should have known Mum was up to something when you showed up at that dinner. Cynthia tried to tell me, but—'

'*I* should have told you, but Mama, she—'

'Shh,' Ade says, pulling her into him. 'It's fine.'

'You're not mad?' she asks him.

'No,' he whispers, holding her more tightly. 'I'm not mad.'

Ife knows she should be relieved, but his non-reaction somehow seems worse. If she'd found out Ade had been meddling in one of her relationships, she would have been furious. So why wasn't he?

'Fey, please, let me in.' Once again, the image of Ade at her door that night flashes in her mind. She lets it play in her head for a little longer this time, before pushing it away.

CHAPTER TWENTY-FIVE

One week before Cynthia's disappearance

After seven years of finding every conceivable excuse to avoid going back home, Cynthia was on the train to Manchester, puffy-eyed and filled with regret.

She'd spent the past week sleeping in Mark's spare bedroom, alternating between hating Ade and seeing reminders of him everywhere. It didn't help that he'd been sending her non-stop WhatsApp messages and voice notes begging her to talk to him.

It was easy to ignore him when Mark was around to keep her company, but since he'd left for Manchester himself a couple of days earlier, Cynthia had found herself looking for ways to excuse Ade's behaviour – it wasn't his fault his mother was insane, he'd actually stood up for her this time, they loved each other, that should be enough. It was this final bit of reasoning that had sent Cynthia on this five-hour journey across the country to spend the bank-holiday weekend with her older sister Valerie and her husband Frank.

Cynthia gazed out of the window as the city skyline gave way to farmland and hills. She'd opted to take the fastest train from Bristol to Manchester and had already messaged Valerie to let her know she was coming home for a couple of days. Busy woman that she was, Valerie had only responded with a thumbs-up emoji.

Cynthia wouldn't go as far as saying she was looking forward to going home, especially because it felt like she had no other choice, but if nothing else it would be nice to see her sister again. The last time they'd met up was in London, just before she moved to Windchapel. She'd grilled her about Ade, trying to suss him out without meeting him, and at the time Cynthia had been so sure about Ade that God himself couldn't have stopped her from moving in with him. How things had changed.

Cynthia's phone vibrated in her hand, and a message from Tayo flashed on the screen.

> Ade's day drinking and am hiding in my room. When you coming home?
>
> your mother tried to poison me, so . . . never?
>
> TBF, he seems pretty torn up about it.
>
> DO NOT DEFEND HIM TAYO.
>
> I aint. He's probs gonna kick me out soon anyways.
>
> he wouldnt dare.
>
> <3

It was early afternoon when the train finally pulled in at Manchester Piccadilly, and Cynthia took a cab straight to Valerie's. She had a bottle of brandy ready when Cynthia arrived, and she pulled her into a much-needed hug.

'Come on, then,' she said, leading Cynthia into her kitchen.

Now that she was home, cuddled by the warmth of her older sister's welcome, the tears she'd been holding back finally resurfaced.

'I'm such an idiot,' she said, dabbing her eye with the back of her finger.

'Aw, hun.' Valerie held her arms out, and Cynthia sank into her embrace, allowing Valerie to carry some of her weight. 'Are you sure he knows you guys broke up?' It was such an unexpected thing for her to say, and Cynthia burst out laughing.

'What?' Valerie pretended to be annoyed by her reaction. 'These bougie boys aren't as smart as they seem, ya know.'

Valerie made them each a cup of black tea and stirred in enough brandy to knock them out.

'The worst thing is,' Cynthia said, taking a sip of her tea then wincing, 'I still love him.'

'Of course you do,' Valerie replied, using the pads of her thumbs to wipe Cynthia's tears away. She felt nineteen again, mad at her father for not allowing to live her life. Mad at her ex-boyfriend Francis for not fighting for them.

Mad at whoever the hell it was who told her father about their relationship.

They'd managed to keep it a secret for almost a year, but then, one night after her father's weekly leadership meeting, she'd received a text from Francis saying, *He knows.*

Cynthia had lain awake all night, waiting for her father to storm into her room, drag her from her bed and give her a verbal lashing. Instead, he'd waited until breakfast the next morning.

As Cynthia sat across from him, her cereal turning soggy, he'd told her that she'd shamed the family, embarrassed him in front of his church, that she was no longer welcome in his house. She'd simply nodded, gone to pack her bags and headed over to Francis, thinking he would take her in. How wrong she'd been.

The moment he opened the door and found her on the other side, he'd freaked out and broken up with her on the spot. Eventually, she'd found herself at Valerie's. Even though she was newly married, she'd taken her sister in without a second thought.

'But you deserve so much better, hun,' Valerie continued, smoothing back Cynthia's hair.

Cynthia frowned. 'Don't say it.'

'What? I didn't say anything.'

'I know what you're thinking.'

No matter what you were going through, Valerie believed

there was no excuse for 'unruly' hair and unkempt clothes, both of which Cynthia was currently sporting.

'At least let me braid it for you.'

'Fine,' Cynthia huffed, but deep down she knew it was exactly what she needed.

They moved into the living room. Valerie sat down on her sofa, and Cynthia settled on the floor between her knees and told her sister everything while she braided her hair.

She recounted Mama's dinner party with the surprise guest while Valerie gently combed out the knots in her hair and applied a leave-in conditioner.

She told her about meeting Mark, and how much he'd helped her, while Valerie parted her hair and greased her scalp.

She only stopped halfway through a plait when Cynthia told her about the incident with the crayfish. She could feel Valerie's hands shaking with anger, and Cynthia thought she heard her mutter *are you fucking kidding me,* but she didn't interrupt.

By the time Valerie had finished, Cynthia had told her the whole sordid tale and actually felt better. In a way, she wished she'd spoken to her sister sooner; she might have managed to avoid the whole debacle in the first place. Although Cynthia rarely listened to her sister when it came to relationships. Maybe that was why they always ended so badly.

Valerie smoothed Cynthia's braids down one last time.

'Done,' she said.

Cynthia felt her hair, and her mouth dropped open.

'What did you do?'

She jumped up from her position on the floor and examined herself in the gold-plated mirror that hung on the wall. A dozen chunky braids fell from her face.

'I look twelve.'

'You'll always be twelve to me, baby girl.' Valerie went in for a hug, but Cynthia manoeuvred out of the way.

'Val, I can't go out like this.'

She cackled.

'Valerie!'

'Relax.' Valerie sipped her brandied tea. 'It'll be a banging braid-out tomorrow, trust.'

Cynthia glanced in the mirror again. She was right. Cynthia had tried to create the mystical braid-out look on more occasions than she cared to admit, but her hair always ended up a frizzy, matted mess. But if anyone could get a braid-out right, it was Valerie. Valerie had always done Cynthia's hair when they were growing up. As much as they loved their mother, neither of them appreciated the uneven cornrows they were forced to wear to school, so Valerie had taught herself how to do different styles and recreated them on Cynthia.

'Where are you going, anyway?' Valerie asked, and

Cynthia shrugged and smiled. Mark had invited her for some much-needed R&R the next day, but she wasn't going to volunteer that information.

'Thank you, by the way.' Cynthia rested her head on Valerie's shoulder, and Valerie rubbed her arm.

'And don't worry about Ade,' Valerie said. 'I never liked his bougie ass anyway.'

'Val!' But Cynthia was laughing as she reprimanded her sister.

'What? I should know. No one's more bougie than me.'

Cynthia looked around the living room, taking in the cream leather sofa covered in cushions and the matching furry rug, and nodded in agreement.

'He fucked up *massively*,' Valerie continued, suddenly serious. 'No one will blame you if you want to walk away. But . . . if you want to forgive him, that's okay too.'

Tears stung Cynthia's eyes again. Valerie was spot-on in her assessment of what was happening in Cynthia's heart.

Ade had treated her horribly, and if it had been someone she knew, she would have told them to cut their losses and get the hell out of there. But this was Ade. Sweet, infuriating, possibly the love of her life Ade. She didn't want to think about what her life would be like without him, so she asked Valerie about her husband, Frank, instead.

'Is he at least coming around to the idea now?'

'I don't know,' she said, grabbing both their mugs and heading back into the kitchen. Cynthia followed behind her. 'Having a baby is a massive decision, and he's worried I'll change my mind again.'

Cynthia scratched the back of her head. It was true, Valerie was notorious for backing out of things last minute, from a simple order at a restaurant right up to marrying Frank. Cynthia had practically had to drag her to the altar that day, leaving Frank panicking for most of the morning.

Valerie had of course taken the plunge, and they were still besotted with each other, but she couldn't blame the guy for questioning Valerie's sincerity.

'And this is definitely what you want?' It was Cynthia's turn to give some sisterly advice. 'You always said you didn't want them, right?'

'I said I wasn't sure.'

'And now you are?'

She nodded. 'A hundred and ten per cent.'

Cynthia hesitated. 'You know once it's done, once it's *here*, you can't change your mind.'

'I'm aware. Don't you think I've thought this through?'

In all honesty, Cynthia hadn't been so sure, but it had been a few months since she'd last spoken to Valerie about having a baby, and she hadn't changed her tune, so maybe that was a good sign.

Cynthia sighed and looked up at her sister, whose expression was desperate for approval. 'You're going to make a great mum,' Cynthia told her, and Valerie glowed.

'I am, aren't I?'

'Just be glad that your in-laws are stateside.'

Valerie gave her sister a sad smile.

'You should go and see Mum and Dad while you're here. They miss you.'

Cynthia shrugged. 'Maybe.' She still hadn't quite forgiven her parents for what they'd done to her all those years ago. Sure, she wouldn't be the successful woman she was today if they hadn't, but it still hurt, how swiftly they'd thrown away their relationship just because she'd done something they didn't approve of.

She had been lucky, *extremely* lucky, that she hadn't ended up homeless, addicted or dead back then. Anything could have happened to her, but all they'd cared about was their precious church and reputation. She could only imagine what they'd say about her 'living in sin' with Ade. Best to avoid the situation altogether.

'Do it,' Valerie insisted. 'Or you'll regret it later.'

They spent the rest of the evening in their pyjamas, downing shots, eating Doritos and tea cakes, and watching horror movies with their heads covered by a blanket.

A movie and a half later, while a masked man with a chainsaw chased a half-naked woman through the woods, something tugged at the blanket, and they both screamed. Frank's spectacled face stared down at them.

'Oh hey, bubba,' Valerie said, reaching for his hand. 'We thought you were a serial killer.'

Frank kissed the top of her head. 'You promised me you weren't going to watch these horror movies anymore. We're going to be up all night now.'

'I certainly hope so.'

Valerie leant in to give him a kiss that was probably more passionate than he was comfortable with in front of guests because when they pulled apart his light-brown skin flushed red. Cynthia felt a pang of jealousy at the intimacy between them. Despite his usual shyness, they were clearly still in love after over a decade of marriage. What was their secret?

'I bought dinner,' he announced, glancing at Cynthia. 'Y'all ready to eat?'

'I'm all right.' Cynthia was in no mood to spend the evening with these lovebirds making goo-goo eyes at each other. 'I think I'll go lie down for a bit.'

'You okay?' Valerie asked, once Frank had left for the kitchen.

'Yeah, just need some space. Go talk to Frank.'

Valerie gave her shoulder a squeeze. 'Wish me luck.'

*

Valerie had kept the bedroom she'd given her exactly the same. It was still decorated in soft colours – muted pinks and pastel greens that evoked the feelings of calm she'd so desperately needed back then, and now. Photos of the two of them were dotted around the room in glittery frames, and Cynthia felt guilty that it had taken her so long to come back here, to the one place that had always been a sanctuary.

Now, she slipped off her jeans, fished her phone from her bag and crawled into the king-sized bed. The sheets were cool against her skin, and she closed her eyes, trying to silence the memory of Mama watching with indifference as she struggled to breathe, of Ade hurling the plates off the table. But no matter how many deeps breaths she took, how much she tossed and turned, she couldn't shake the thoughts from her mind. And so she did what any desperate, insomnia-ridden millennial would do, and turned on her phone.

Big mistake.

Valerie had deliberately kept her occupied enough not to look at her phone for the majority of the day. Otherwise she might have given in and done something stupid, like accidently liking one of Ade's pandering Instagram posts. But now she was alone, unable to get to sleep, her phone was all she had left. And so, she gave in and looked. A dozen missed calls and at least thirty messages from Ade, most of them a variation of please babe and I'm sorry, come home. The last one he'd sent, just under an hour earlier, was more desperate, though: If you don't respond, I'll have to come and get you. She was glad she hadn't told him she was going to Manchester.

ffs ade just leave it. we'll talk soon okay?

When? xxxx

She was about to fling her phone across the room when it rang.

'Welcome home,' Mark said. 'You still up for hanging out tomorrow?'

There was music in the background and people talking. Maybe he was at a party.

'Sure,' Cynthia replied.

'Great, I'll pick you up at eight.'

'Wait, don't you need my—?'

But Mark had already hung up.

CHAPTER TWENTY-SIX

Ife, present day

'Where is my son?'

Mama pushes her way through the front door, bringing the cold in with her. It had snowed the night before, and muddy water pools on Ife's freshly washed floors. She's been cleaning a lot lately, scrubbing and hoovering, dusting and polishing, but the house still feels dirty somehow.

In the days since Detective Callaghan's interrogation, she has given up searching for clues, given up trying to find out what happened to Cynthia. It doesn't matter anyway. Ade already knows that Mama tried to use her to break him and Cynthia up, but he doesn't seem to care. The apparitions seem to have gone too. For two days in a row, she has woken up to a tidy house. Her clothes have stayed in her wardrobe, and the ring is nowhere to be found. Everything is as normal as it can be. She is happy, *they* are happy – and yet, Ife can't stop thinking about the night Ade showed up at her flat unannounced. His frantic knocking, his bloodshot eyes, his desperate words.

Marry me, Fey.

At the time, she'd seen that desperation as a sign of his love. A sign that he'd finally realised the depth of what they had. But what if she'd been wrong? What if something else had been going on?

It doesn't help that Mark hasn't stopped texting and calling, asking her if she's found anything, if they can meet again. If she responds, it will only encourage him further, so she has taken to deleting his messages as soon as they come through. As for Ade himself . . .

'There was an emergency at the office, so he had to go in,' Ife replies to Mama's question, trying to block her path into the house. 'But I'll let him know you came.'

Mama pulls off her faux-fur jacket and piles it into Ife's arms. 'What is wrong with you? So you don't have time for your mother-in-law again? After all I have done for you.'

She pushes past Ife and into the living room.

'Peace be unto this house,' she says, before making herself comfortable on the sofa. 'Ifelayo, must I ask you for a cup of tea?'

'No, Mama,' Ife says. She goes into the kitchen and returns with a tea set and a plate of custard cream biscuits. She kneels next to Mama to make her tea: milk first, tea, then two teaspoons of sugar. Ife stirs it and hands it over to Mama on a saucer. Mama takes a sip and sighs.

'You have always been a good tea maker,' Mama tells her. 'Oya come and sit down.' Mama pats the seat next to her, and Ife does as she is told. This isn't the first time Ife and Mama have had tea together.

Growing up, Mama had been like a second mother to her. As much as she loved the aunty who'd taken her in when she moved to England as a child, her career as a nurse had often got in the way of her parenting. Mama had taken it upon herself to look out for her, treating her as the daughter she never got to have. It was why Ife had trusted her when she invited her to dinner the night she found out about Ade and Cynthia. Why Ife had been so surprised when she learned it had all been part of Mama's grand plan to destroy their relationship.

'What is wrong, my dear?' Mama observes Ife with concern. 'You are being very quiet today. How are things with Adebayo?'

Despite everything Mama has done, Ife finds herself wanting to confide in her. All this time she's had no one to talk to, no one to support her, and she knows that at the very least Mama understands what she's going through.

And so, leaving out the parts about Mark, she tells Mama about the text messages, the break-ins, Detective Callaghan's visit.

'What did she say?' Mama asks.

'She knew I'd gone to the spa that day and thought it might have something to do with what happened to

Cynthia. Ade told her he'd planned the whole thing, and that was that.'

'And what of my son? Are they still suspecting him?'

'I don't know.' Ife sighs.

Mama takes a sip of her tea.

'The Lord is your strength, my dear,' she says. 'Let me pray for you.'

Ife shakes her head.

'What we did was wrong,' she says, finally saying the words she should have said months ago. When she'd called Mama the day after that horrible dinner, outraged by her deception, Mama had shrugged her off and insisted that she was only trying to give her what she'd always wanted.

'Do you not still love him?' Mama had asked her at the time, as if this somehow absolved her of how she'd treated Cynthia. If Ife had known that Mama was trying to meddle in Ade's relationship, she probably wouldn't have agreed to go.

'I do,' Ife had replied. 'But . . .'

Mama had kissed her teeth. 'This is the problem with you young people, no forward thinking. How can you let someone just block your blessings like that? You will see. Once we are done with her, you and Ade will be free to be together as God intended. Soon you will be thanking me.'

'I don't want any part in this, aunty.'

Mama had scoffed, and Ife could practically hear her rolling her eyes over the phone.

'You think you have a choice after tonight? You think I won't tell him that it was your idea to have this dinner? After you have been flaunting yourself in front of him, who do you think he will believe? I know my son. He will never forgive you.'

Ife had sighed. Considering how far Mama had already gone to rope her into her plan, Ife knew she would have no problem lying to save herself. Even if Ife called Ade first and tried to explain, he might think she'd been part of it from the beginning, and she didn't want to risk that. If the dinner had shown her anything, besides the fact that Mama had clearly lost the plot, it was that she had missed Ade's easy company, the warm weight of his friendship. Dubai had been lonely, and then she'd been forced to come back home to no job, and even fewer friends. Ade was offering to fix all of that.

'Fine, but—'

'Good.' Mama had hung up before Ife could finish her sentence.

After their phone call, Ife didn't hear from Mama for weeks, had thought she had given up on her ridiculous plan.

But then, one night, Mama had called her and told her to book herself into Wild Cherry Spa. According to her, Ade had planned a spa day for Cynthia so he and Mama could spend some time alone together, and she wanted Ife to sow seeds of doubt in Cynthia's mind.

'You and Ade are working together, abi? Make her think the two of you are having an affair.'

Ife hadn't bothered to protest, didn't think she needed to. She would go to the spa, make nice with Cynthia, and tell Mama she'd done her best to come between the couple but it hadn't worked. And that would be that. She could even make the booking, send Mama a screenshot, and then not go.

But the night before she was due to go to the spa, Mama had called her and told her there'd been a change of plan.

'When she isn't looking, I want you to take something from her, just like she has taken my son from me.'

'No.' Ife shook her head, even though she knew Mama couldn't see her. 'Aunty, this is too much. I'll talk to her, but I'm not taking her stuff.'

There was a pause, and for one naive moment, Ife had thought that Mama was going to drop it.

'Ah, so you have grown wings?' Mama said instead. 'Okay. Let me just find that picture you sent me of your booking. I'm sure Ade would be intrigued to see it.'

Ife could hear Mama tapping her phone, and she winced, unsure of what to say.

She didn't want to do any of this, knew it was wrong, but she was in too deep – not just with Mama, but with Ade.

Since they'd started working together, they'd grown close again, and yes, she still had feelings for him, and sure, maybe he and Cynthia weren't the best match, but it was more than that.

In the time they'd been apart, he'd matured. Had become the friend she'd always needed him to be: kind, playful, attentive. It was healing something within her. The part that had shattered when Demi died. Even if they couldn't be together, she still wanted him in her life. Needed him. And so, when Cynthia had gone to use the bathroom, leaving her bag in her care, Ife had dug out her purse and slipped one of her bank cards into her pocket. She'd hoped that it was a card that Cynthia didn't use often, that it would take a while for her to notice, but then Mama had shown up on her doorstep in floods of tears. At first, Ife had thought Ade had found out about their thievery and was horrified to learn that Mama had essentially poisoned Cynthia.

'You could have killed her.'

Mama had scoffed through her tears, had insisted that Cynthia had been pretending, that she was trying to make her look bad so she could get rid of her and have Ade all to herself. She went on about how she wasn't done with Cynthia yet, had sworn to *put that foolish girl back in her place*. As Ife listened to Mama's rant, she remembered Cynthia's unexpected toast at the spa and immediately felt ashamed. She'd been a terrible friend to Ade, had almost become an accomplice to murder. She'd told Mama right then that she was welcome to stay the night, but she was done helping her, even if she told Ade everything.

'What do you mean by *we*?' Mama says now, placing her teacup on the stool in front of her. 'Of course, it is terrible what happened to that poor girl, may her soul rest in peace. But everything I did was to protect my son. You, Ifelayo, were selfishly pursuing your own carnal desires. You didn't care what happened to my son, or that girl, or anybody else but yourself. You are the one who decided to take it too far. So, there is no *we* here, oh, Ifelayo, there is only you. And only you can bear the consequences of what you have done.'

Apparently satisfied with her speech, Mama returns to drinking her tea, while Ife tries to shake off Mama's accusations. She was the one who had hated Cynthia, who had plotted and planned against her. She was the one who'd forced Ife to go to the spa, to steal her card, and even then her plan hadn't worked. Now that Cynthia is dead, she's blaming Ife for the whole thing.

'Ifelayo.' Next to her, Mama has suddenly gone very still. She is staring into her cup as if the Devil himself is in there. 'Kí léléyì?'

'Mama?' Ife leans over to peer into Mama's cup, and there, floating at the top, is Cynthia's ring.

'How did this get inside my drink? It was not here before.'

'I . . . I . . . I—'

'You are a witch!' Mama jumps to her feet. Her cup smashes on the floor, spilling tea, and ceramic and, of course, Cynthia's ring. 'God help me, oh.' Mama looks to the ceiling, rubbing her hands together in prayer. 'My son has married a witch.'

'Mama, I'm not a—'

'Blood of Jesus.' Mama bends to remove one of her shoes and lifts it threateningly. 'Get out of this house.'

'Mama, please. Let me—'

Mama takes a swing at her, and Ife just about manages to block it.

'I said, get out of this house.'

Mama tries to hit her again, and again and again, and Ife runs for cover behind the sofa. 'I warned you,' she continues, 'that if you did not leave my son alone, I would deal with you. You didn't listen. I reported your behaviour to the police, you still did not want to hear—'

'What?'

Mama freezes, shoe mid-air, at the sound of Ade's voice.

'Adebayo. Thank God you are home. Your . . . your . . . your wife.' Mama points an accusing shoe at Ife. 'She is a witch.'

Ade casts a weary glance at Ife, who slowly stands from behind the sofa where she'd been cowering. He looks tired and furious.

'What did you just say?' he asks Mama. 'About the police.'

Mama stays silent, and Ade loses it.

'Again, Mum,' he shouts. 'Again. How many people have to lose their fucking lives before you stop this. First it was Cynthia who was bad for me, and now it's Ife . . . Ife, who I've known my whole life, who you've always liked. But now we're married, and suddenly she's a witch.'

'Ah, Adebayo, no.' Mama tries to defend herself. 'I . . . I was drinking my tea. And . . . and then . . .'

Mama shifts the direction of her shoe so that it's pointing at the mess on the floor. The shattered cup and spilt tea are just as she left them, but the ring is no longer there.

'Yeh,' Mama jumps back. 'Where did it go?'

Mama glares at Ife, as if she'd been the one to make it disappear.

'Mum, you need to leave,' Ade tells her.

'Adebayo.'

'No,' he says firmly. 'Even after what you did to Cynthia, I gave you another chance. I thought it would be different with Fey, but now I see it had nothing to do with Cynthia and everything to do with you trying to control me. Well, I'm done. I won't let you keep ruining my life. As far as I'm concerned, I am no longer your son.'

CHAPTER TWENTY-SEVEN

Ife, present day

'I need to tell you something,' Ade says later that evening as they sit cuddled together on the sofa.

When Mama left, Ife had gone straight to the kitchen to make dinner, and they'd sat in silence as they ate and watched the news. Ife had thought that Ade was quiet because he didn't want to talk about what had just happened with his mother, but now it seems he has more bad news.

'What's up?' she asks him, keeping her tone light even though she is already panicking.

Ade sighs and then falls silent again. He looks down and starts picking at his fingernails.

'Dey,' she gently prompts him. 'What's wrong?'

'I got pushed out of my company today,' he says, refusing to look at her. 'They called me in just to kick me out. Claimed that Cynthia's death and my arrest have tarnished our reputation. It's my *fucking* company.' Ade slams his fist against his leg, and Ife winces on his behalf. 'Anyway, I thought you should know.'

He returns his attention to the television and raises the volume. Ife grabs the remote from his hand and turns it off.

'Aren't you going to fight this?'

Ade looks at her then, and his resigned expression tells her everything she needs to know.

'There's nothing I can do except take the payout,' he says.

'Have you spoken to Robert?'

'Robert can't help me, Ife.' It sounds as if he isn't just talking about his business. 'You should probably start looking for a new job, too.'

She wants to tell him that it'll be okay, that they'll be fine, but with a baby on the way and two unemployed parents, there's only so much hope she can have, especially when Ade has already given up.

'Maybe just give him a call. See what he says,' she tries again.

'There's no point,' he says, shaking his head. 'Besides, it's what I deserve. I'm just sorry I dragged you into this.' He gestures for the remote, and Ife reluctantly hands it back to him.

It's not like him to give up so easily and yet now he's blaming himself for something they both know he didn't do. It feels strange, and Ife decides right then to resume her search for the truth. His strange behaviour, his outburst at Mama, and now this, all make it seem like he knows more than he's letting on. Since his arrest, she's been worried that he was the one who killed Cynthia – but maybe all this time he was protecting someone else.

CHAPTER TWENTY-EIGHT

One week before Cynthia's disappearance

'Turn around again,' Valerie said, the following evening.

'No.' Cynthia applied a touch more lip gloss for good measure, and Valerie's eyebrows shot up.

'You looking to kiss someone with those lips?'

'Just you, my love.'

'Why would you say such a horrible thing?'

She fluffed the back of Cynthia's hair and smiled at her in the mirror. As promised, her braid-out had turned out beautifully. Coily spirals formed a mane around her head, and Cynthia was impressed by how healthy her hair was looking. She usually kept it tied up in a bun of twists or an Afro puff, so it was nice to see that the small fortune she was spending on natural hair products wasn't completely in vain.

'So, where's this Mark guy taking you?'

'Some music thing.' Cynthia shrugged. 'One of his clients has a gig at Midnight Blues, and he asked if I wanted to come along.'

'Mm-hmm.'

'It's not like that.' Cynthia studied her outfit in the mirror. Her silver halterneck dress fell well above her knees, and she'd coupled it with a pair of matching silver heels. 'He's hung up on some other woman. Basically blew up his marriage for her.'

She had to admit, she was looking forward to going out. To doing something other than dodging Ade's calls and text messages, which hadn't died down despite the fact that she'd already told him she'd go and see him later in the week, once she was back in Windchapel. Which reminded her, she needed to send Mark Valerie's address. She grabbed her phone from the bed and shot Mark a message.

'You'll be fine,' Valerie said, catching Cynthia's frown. 'Just look at that dress.'

Cynthia flipped her hair with her hand. 'I know, right?'

'You're all grown up, little sis.'

'It's only natural.'

'If only Dad could see you now.'

Cynthia rolled her eyes. 'Don't start.'

'You should give him a call. Go see him while you're here.'

'I'm not his prodigal daughter, Valerie. I don't want or need his approval.'

'I know, but—'

'But nothing, Val. If he wants to talk to me, he has my number.'

The doorbell rang. Cynthia was so eager to get away from the conversation that she barely registered how quickly Mark had arrived.

'We'll talk more later,' Valerie said, giving Cynthia a hug. 'Go make Ade jealous.'

Mark had sent a chauffeur to pick her up, and when she slid inside the car, there was a bottle of champagne and an envelope waiting for her.

Enjoy. I don't do this often. M x

Cynthia smiled. She knew Mark had acquired some wealth from a handful of indie hits he'd produced, as well as his investments, but he rarely flaunted it. The fact that he was doing this for her made her feel warm inside. Whoever his secret woman was, she was one lucky lady.

With a satisfied sigh, Cynthia poured herself a glass of champagne and sat back on the plush leather seat. An R&B song she didn't recognise emerged from the speakers, and she asked the driver if it was one of Mark's.

'Yes madam, the whole album,' he replied. 'He asked me to play it. Thought you might like it.'

Twenty minutes later, they parked outside Midnight Blues, an intimate music venue Cynthia used to dream of gigging at.

A woman in a little black dress and no shoes took her name and told her to go down the flight of stairs and turn left. The walls that led to the basement had photos of artists that had played there, some of them well known. Cynthia felt a pang of nostalgia at what could have been.

The room was dimly lit, with fairy lights scattered all

around. A musician was on stage singing with her guitar, a dozen or so people standing in front of the stage waving their arms to the music.

On the other side of the room was a bar and several red padded booths, most of which were empty. Cynthia made her way over to them, all the while scanning the darkness for Mark. She spotted him engrossed in conversation at the bar. Cynthia slid into one of the booths and texted him to let him know that she'd arrived. She watched him as he took his phone out of his pocket and read the message. His head shot up, and he looked left and right until his eyes finally settled on hers. Cynthia gave him a little finger wave. He said something to the woman he was speaking to and made his way over.

'You made it,' he said, settling into the seat opposite her.

'Nice touch with the chauffeur,' she told him. 'Thank you.'

Mark smiled shyly, shifting in his seat, and Cynthia felt his knee accidentally brushing hers under the table. 'I figured you deserved a treat after everything that's happened.'

'Yeah, well . . .' Cynthia let her words drift off, not wanting to talk about Ade. 'You look good, by the way. Never thought I'd ever see you in an actual shirt.'

Mark had swapped his usual uniform of Crocs and a hoodie for a dark-blue dress shirt and loafers.

'I try,' he said, his smile unwavering. 'Ready to dance?' Mark stood and held out his hand. Cynthia took it and let him lead her to a corner near the stage.

'Wow,' Mark whispered when he caught sight of her outfit, and Cynthia felt her face heat up. Normally she would have said something innocent yet flirty, but suddenly she was feeling shy.

'He's good, isn't he?' Mark said, nodding towards the musician who'd replaced the woman playing when Cynthia had arrived.

'Mmm.' Cynthia nodded. His voice was soulful, but she couldn't get behind the lyrics. 'Not my kind of thing, but yeah.'

'Go on . . . what's your type of music then?'

'It's not the music per se,' Cynthia mused. 'He just seems really naive. All that talk about everlasting love.'

Mark gave her a sad smile. 'Still haven't spoken to Ade?'

'He's tried, but . . . I guess I'm not ready to face him yet.'

'Understandable. All me and Emma do when we get together is fight.'

Cynthia considered asking him about his mystery woman, but she couldn't bring herself to do it. He'd already told her that he hadn't had an affair, and she didn't want to offend him. Instead, she asked him where his bracelets were.

'Oh,' Mark looked down at his bare wrist and shrugged.

'I don't usually wear them in this crowd. Most people don't get it.'

He closed the space between them so that they were almost touching. Something unspeakable sizzled between them. To Cynthia's surprise, Mark began undoing the top button of his shirt. She moved to stop him, to tell him not here, but then she caught sight of the black necklace he was trying to show her.

'Obsidian,' he said, rubbing the rock between his fingers. 'It's one thing to wear it for show, it's quite another to actually believe in this stuff. So, when I'm not home' – he tilted his head – 'Windchapel home . . . I keep it under wraps.'

They both returned their attention to the musician, who was slowing down his set, the heavy drums making way for the piano. Couples and strangers cuddled together. Mark gestured for her to come closer, and Cynthia slipped into his arms. He placed his hands gently on her hips, and Cynthia rested her head on his shoulder, letting the music transport her away from the party, away from Mark, to a place she'd rather not go. Where she and Ade were dancing, just like this, on a beach, at a wedding, at a concert.

Even though Ade hated dancing, was too self-conscious to really enjoy it, he had always indulged her. She would miss that about him, his willingness to look like a damn fool for her. Those moments had become fewer and fewer, especially in the past few months. But in the early days, he would have done almost anything for her. She wanted that Ade back, but she worried that he was long gone.

'I'm glad you're okay,' Mark whispered in her ear. The hairs on the back of her neck and arms prickled. 'And I'm glad you came. This would have been a lot less fun without you.'

The music fell away, and so did Mark's arms.

'I'll be back,' Mark told her. 'Don't go anywhere.'

Not wanting to stand there alone, Cynthia went to get herself a drink.

'Blue Lagoon?' the bartender asked.

'How did you—?'

'Mark. He told me to keep them coming.'

Cynthia accepted the drink, vaguely wondering how Mark had guessed what she would like.

As she sipped, her thoughts returned to Ade, who almost always needed to be reminded of what tea to buy. She'd messaged him earlier and agreed to have dinner with him at the house in a few days' time. Mark was meeting with the potential studio investors then too, and she wanted to be in the area just in case they wanted to talk to her. She was already dreading dinner with Ade, but she knew it had to be done, that she needed to put this chapter of her life to rest. It was time to move on.

Someone tapped her shoulder.

'Holy crap. It *is* you.'

Cynthia squinted at the man in front of her. He was dressed casually in dark jeans and a bomber jacket, his short twists falling over one side of his face in a fringe. But it was his dark-brown eyes, familiar yet somehow older, that were most recognisable.

'Francis?'

The last time she'd seen him, he'd been breaking up with her to please his pastor, her father. A wave of betrayal washed over her, catching her off guard. She had thought she'd forgiven him, thought that she'd moved on from the hurt. So why did she feel like she was nineteen years old again?

'Ah, so you do remember me,' he said, looking pleased with himself. His voice was still the same. R&B smooth with a little bit of bass to it. He'd been a good singer back then too, although he'd never expressed a desire to pursue music professionally. 'I heard you went down to London to make a name for yourself. And now you're back, yeah?'

'I'm just here visiting my sister,' Cynthia said, trying to see if she could spot Mark. He was back at the bar, talking to the same woman he was with earlier. Cynthia stared at him, willing him with her eyes to look up.

'Valerie, right? I saw her at church the other day.'

Cynthia returned her attention to him.

'You still go?'

'Yeah, well.' Francis rubbed the back of his neck, looking guilty. 'I sacrificed a lot for it. Everything, really.'

Cynthia could feel an apology coming on, and she snuck another glance at Mark, who finally looked up. She gave him a 'help me' look, and he held up a finger to let her know he'd be there in a minute.

'Oh, you're here with someone,' Francis said, following her gaze. 'Some of the old gang are here too.' Francis pointed in the opposite direction, to a group of three sitting in one of the booths. 'You can join us if you like. They'd love to see you.'

'Heeey.' Mark arrived just in time, placing a warm hand on Cynthia's bare shoulder and pulling her close.

'Mark, this is Francis. Francis . . . Mark.'

Mark stuck out his hand. 'Nice to meet you.' But Francis just stared at him, confused.

'Chris?' he said. 'I didn't know you two were together.'

'Excuse me?' Mark looked at Francis, really looked at him, and then suddenly went pale.

'I'm sorry,' he said slowly. 'I'm not sure what you mean?'

'Wait, do you two know each other?' Cynthia asked, looking from one to the other.

'No,' Mark said, before Francis, who was looking at her like she'd lost her mind, could respond. 'Actually,' Mark continued, glancing down at his phone. 'We need to go.'

He pulled Cynthia away, almost tugging off her arm in

the process, dragging her back up the stairs. Despite Cynthia's protest that he was hurting her, he didn't stop until they were outside.

The car park was dark, except for a few street lights which were just starting to come on.

'What the hell was that about?' Cynthia rubbed her sore arm.

'Sorry,' Mark replied. 'I completely forgot I need to be somewhere else. Come on, I'll drop you home.'

He was lying, of course he was lying, but Cynthia couldn't understand why.

'How do you know Francis?'

'I don't.'

'It seems like he knows you.'

'I guess I have one of those faces.'

'Why did he call you Chris?'

'I don't know.'

'Mark.'

'Cynthia.' His laugh was strained. 'It's fine. Happens to me all the time. I bet there's a guy out there called Chris who's just as frustrated as I am.'

Mark unlocked his car and opened the passenger door for her.

'You coming?'

'Not until you tell me the truth.'

Anger flashed across his face.

'I've told you everything,' he said. 'And I'm not going to stand here and let you accuse me of being a liar.'

'I'm not—'

'Good,' Mark interrupted. 'Then drop it, and let's go.'

When Cynthia didn't move, Mark slammed the car door shut.

'Fine, you can walk. Or better yet, get Francis to take you.'

He got into the driver's seat and slammed that door too. The engine roared to life.

'Why are you being like this?'

'Last chance, Cynthia.'

'Just tell me the truth. I promise I won't get mad.'

At that, Mark pulled out of his parking space and sped away, leaving Cynthia alone in the car park.

CHAPTER TWENTY-NINE

Ife, present day

Ife is late. As she sneaks in through the door of Nyara's café, she spots an older man on the makeshift stage at the back, reading a passage from the Bible.

She knows she shouldn't be here, knows she doesn't belong here amongst Cynthia's mourners, but sitting at home waiting for either her or Ade to get arrested is no longer an option, especially now that Ade has been removed from his company and she is likely on her way out too.

Someone here, amongst Cynthia's closest friends and family, must know something about what happened to her in the lead-up to her disappearance, to her murder.

And so, Ife makes a beeline to the only empty seat in a row of teenagers then scans the room for someone she might know.

Nyara is sitting adjacent to the stage, managing the music system which has been moved from its previous spot. The stage itself has become the pulpit for Cynthia's memorial – the tables have been covered with bouquets of lilies, photographs of Cynthia placed carefully between them. There's one of Cynthia as a baby, as a teenager singing in what looks like a church choir, and several of her as an adult dancing on stage.

Besides Nyara, Ife doesn't spot anyone she recognises. She was hoping that at the very least Mark would be here so she could ask him a few more questions.

All she knows is that she has to do *something*. And yet now she's here, the thought of trying to weasel information from a bunch of strangers, of people in mourning, suddenly seems ridiculous.

The man on stage takes a seat, and a younger woman who introduces herself as Cynthia's sister takes his place. She sobs all the way through her speech and eventually breaks down completely. A different man helps her to her seat, and Ife is left with the sense that she has done the right thing coming here. Just like her, Cynthia's friends and family want justice.

A few more people give tearful speeches, and then, to Ife's surprise, Tayo appears on stage holding a painting of Cynthia, his hands shaking. Ife slides down in her seat hoping he doesn't spot her as he describes how Cynthia had been like a sister to him, the person he'd looked up to most in the world, the one who'd always supported him. He doesn't explain how he knew her, and Ife doesn't blame him. Considering the initial commotion around Ade's arrest, it makes sense that he doesn't want to advertise he's the main suspect's brother, just like she doesn't want to reveal she's his wife.

Tayo finishes his speech and places the painting of Cynthia in an empty stand behind him. When he turns around, his eyes lock onto hers. Surprise, then confusion, pass over his face but just as quickly disappear as he rushes back to his seat without acknowledging her.

Later, once the service is over, Ife finds herself standing alone in a corner, holding a plate of food someone has handed to her but she hasn't been able to eat from. Nyara is busy attending to the guests, and Ife doesn't want to disturb her. Instead, she makes her way towards the small group congregating by the flowers, rehearsing her questions in her head.

As she gets closer, a woman wearing a black headscarf gives the man standing next to her a hug, and Ife loses her nerve. She isn't a detective; she can't do this. Unable to find a bin, she drops her plate on a nearby table. As she turns to leave, Tayo approaches her, his expression sad but curious.

'I didn't expect to see you here,' he says. His tone is more questioning than judgemental, but telling him the truth, that she thinks Ade is trying to protect their murdering mother, doesn't seem like a good idea.

'I didn't realise the two of you were so close,' she says instead, and Tayo rubs his eyes with the back of his hand.

'Yeah, we were,' he sniffs. 'She always had my back no matter what.' Ife wonders if she's imagining the note of accusation in his voice. Although she's known Tayo for most of his life, she can't even say that she's been a friend to him. Cynthia, meanwhile, had probably only known him for a couple of years, and she'd been like a sister to him. 'I wouldn't even be doing my uni course if it wasn't for her.'

'I'm sorry,' Ife says. 'For everything.'

Tayo looks down at the floor. 'Ade should be here,' he continues. 'It's messed up how the police are painting this picture of him as some jealous ex-boyfriend.'

'You don't think he . . .' It is a relief to finally talk to someone who doesn't think Ade is guilty.

'Nah, man. Ade could never—' He side-eyes her. 'Do you?'

'No, of course not, but—'

'It's crazy. Can you believe they questioned me too? Showed up at my uni accusing me of having an affair with her. Apparently, they found some text messages that seemed suspicious. Forget the fact that I was literally trying to defend him when they broke up.'

A feeling of dread crawls up Ife's back.

'I thought he broke up with her.'

'Is that what he told you?'

Ife opens her mouth to respond, but Tayo shakes his head.

'Not here,' he says, and nods towards the back door.

They make their way outside, where the cold crisp air is disturbed by the smell of rubbish.

Tayo lets out a deep breath and shakes his head again.

'I can't believe he didn't tell you that Mum basically poisoned C's food.'

Tayo's voice is unstable as he shakes his head in disbelief, and Ife feels sick. She'd known what Mama had done and yet did nothing to stop her from going further.

'Do you think . . . ?' Ife asks.

'No,' Tayo says, breathing into his hands to keep them warm. 'Mum's a menace, but I don't think she could . . . I mean, I hope she wouldn't go that far.'

Except she *had* gone that far. It just hadn't worked. Not that time at least.

'Then who?'

Tayo shrugs. 'That's what I've been trying to figure out myself. Maybe it wasn't anyone we know. Maybe it was a random attack. According to the police, she died before she was put in the water.'

Ife shakes her head, trying to rattle the image from her mind, replacing it with her conversation with Mark, the photographs in his living room, his declaration of love. 'Did you know she started seeing someone else after she and Ade broke up?'

'Really? She never said anything to me about it. But I guess that would be kinda weird, right?'

'It was some guy called Mark.' Ife waits to see if the name rings a bell, but Tayo's expression remains unchanged. 'Apparently she was living with him before she disappeared.'

'Oh, *that* guy. Nah, I don't think they had a thing. He had a spare room above Cynthia's studio and let her stay there while she figured things out with Ade. Sorry,' he adds, catching Ife's disappointed expression. 'It's just my understanding of it.'

'It's fine,' Ife says, waving her feelings away. Just because Ade and Cynthia were figuring things out didn't mean that they were getting back together, that Ade's proposal hadn't been genuine.

'Wait, do you think this Mark breda has something to do with this?'

'I don't know anymore,' Ife says. 'Nothing's making sense.'

'Well,' Tayo says, nodding in the direction of Cynthia's studio. 'We know where he lives. Let's go find out.'

'Uh, let's not.' Considering the fact that Ife has been ignoring Mark's messages for the past couple of days, she doubts he'll be all that happy if she shows up at his apartment with the brother of his whatever-Cynthia-was-to-him's ex. And if Mark has been lying to her all this time, then they could be putting themselves in danger.

Except Mark can't be dangerous. All this time, he's been trying to help her, and instead of listening, she's been ignoring him. Besides, he deserves answers too, perhaps even more than Ife.

But before Ife has a chance to say any of this to Tayo, he is already heading down the street.

CHAPTER THIRTY

One week before Cynthia's disappearance

An hour later, after Cynthia had finally managed to get an Uber back to Valerie's, Mark was sitting on the wall outside her house. When she approached him, he at least had the decency to look ashamed.

'What are you doing here? Oh wait, I forgot, you don't answer questions.'

'Okay, I deserved that.' He slipped his hands into his coat pockets. 'I'm sorry for flipping out.'

Cynthia tried to sidestep him to get to the house, but he blocked her way.

'Excuse me,' she said.

'Not until you hear me out.'

'Are you going to tell me the truth this time?'

He let out a pained breath. 'There's no truth to tell.'

She knew he was lying, and his words stung.

'I thought we were friends.'

'We are.' He placed a hand on her shoulder. 'But my life here is complicated. I just got divorced. I have legal bills coming out of every orifice. And my ex-wife is delusional. I don't want you involved in any of that.'

All of that was probably true, but Cynthia didn't know what that had to do with Francis. She told him this, and he frowned.

'I mean . . . it's possible he knows my ex-wife,' he said. 'She's always liked to call me by my middle name, even though I hate it.'

'So your name *is* Chris.'

'No. And if you start calling me that, Cynthia, I swear to God—'

'All right, all right. But why didn't you just say that in the first place?'

Mark shrugged. 'This was meant to be a fun night for both of us. I didn't want to ruin it with my ex-wife drama.'

'Yeah, I get it,' Cynthia said, even though she still felt a little unsure. Still, he'd been a good friend to her these past few months, and he had no reason to lie to her.

'So, I'm forgiven?'

'Fine,' she said. 'But—'

Before she could finish her sentence, she was in his arms. He was holding her so tightly, like he would never let go.

CHAPTER THIRTY-ONE

Ife, present day

'I don't think this is a good idea,' Ife whispers. 'Maybe we should—'

'Chill,' Tayo interrupts her. 'You want to help Ade, don't you?'

Ife sighs in agreement.

'Then let's go talk to the guy. It's not like we're accusing him of anything. We just want to know what he knows.'

Ife huffs. 'Fine, but let me talk to him. He's kind of . . . sensitive.' Ife observes Tayo for a moment. 'And don't tell him you're Ade's brother.'

'Wait, so you proper know this guy?'

'Not really.'

Ife follows Tayo up the flight of stairs that leads to Mark's apartment. He knocks on the door, but Mark doesn't answer. He knocks again. Still no answer. He lifts his fist to knock a third time, but Ife glares at him. He grins that Dolapo grin she knows all too well from Ade, drops his hand and tries the door handle.

Just like last time, the door is unlocked.

Tayo pushes it open and makes his way inside, leaving Ife with no choice but to follow.

'Rah, this guy's bare messy,' Tayo says, as he takes in the chaos in Mark's living room and kitchen. It's nowhere near as tidy as it was when Ife had visited a week earlier. The floor is littered with what look like women's clothes, and that sinking feeling Ife gets every time she has to clear clothes from her own living room returns. Ife isn't sure if this means he is innocent or guilty. If this is all somehow for her benefit.

The photographs by the fireplace have been left untouched, and Tayo climbs over a pile of clothes to get to them. Ife watches him as he studies the one in his hand.

'Check this out,' he says, handing her the photo frame before picking up another one. 'They're fake,' he says. 'They've all been photoshopped.'

Ife looks down at the photograph in her hand, and, just as before, she gets the sense that something is off but she can't quite figure out what.

'Yeah, this guy's sick. I remember this one from C's Instagram. He's morphed his head onto Ade's body.' He places it back on the mantelpiece and wipes his hands on his trousers.

'Did you hear that?' Ife asks, dropping her voice at the sound of something clattering in the distance. 'I think someone's here.'

'Hello? Mark?' Tayo calls out. 'It's better if he thinks we're here to see him,' he whispers. She's never known Tayo to be so brave.

When no one answers, they make their way through the arched entryway that leads to the rest of the apartment.

'Hello,' Tayo calls again. 'You check this room,' he tells her, pointing to the door directly in front of them. 'And I'll take the one up there.'

Heart pounding, Ife says a silent prayer and opens the door just as Tayo instructed. No Mark, but the mess in what appears to be a music studio is even worse than in the living room.

Here, there are papers scattered all over Mark's desk, along with more photoshopped pictures of him and Cynthia. Something clicks in Ife's mind. Cynthia's clothes, the photographs in her own living room, the ring. She'd thought they'd been put there to scare her away, but what if she's missing something?

And then Ife sees it: a ruby-red notebook shining through a sea of white.

She picks it up, starts to flick through it, unsure of what to make of its contents, of the fact that Cynthia's name is on nearly every page.

A door closes behind her, and Ife's stomach dips. She places the journal back on the table and turns to face him.

'Mark,' she says, trying to hold her faltering smile in place. 'Hi.'

CHAPTER THIRTY-TWO

One day before Cynthia's disappearance

'Just go in there and rip the band-aid off, hun,' Valerie told Cynthia over the phone. 'Trust me, you'll feel a thousand times better afterwards.'

Cynthia stared at the home she'd thought she'd spend the rest of her life in and sighed. 'He's such an arsehole for doing this.'

'This' was the dinner she'd agreed to have with Ade so he would leave her alone while she was in Manchester. Now that she was back, she had no choice but to hold up her end of the deal.

'Yeah, well, you can't really blame the guy for trying,' Valerie said. 'It'll be over soon. Call me when it's done.'

Cynthia grabbed her handbag, checked her make-up in the mirror one last time and slammed her car door shut.

The front door was another matter entirely. It had only been a few weeks since she'd left, but she couldn't decide if she should let herself in or ring the doorbell.

She fiddled with her key in her bag, letting the rough edges scratch the pads of her fingers. She took it out, watched it dangle from its key ring, before putting it back into her bag and pressing the bell. It was better this way. Better for her to keep her distance until she'd made her decision.

The door opened, and Cynthia felt an unexpected pang in her chest when she saw him standing there, looking so unsure of himself. It was the first time in three years they'd spent any real time apart, and even when they had, it hadn't been because they were fighting.

Seeing him here, now, she realised that despite everything, despite his psychopathic mother and non-existent backbone, she had missed him. She didn't know how she was going to do this when she still loved him so damn much.

Ade, always optimistic, opened his arms for a hug, and, unable to reject him, she leant into him, giving his waist a gentle squeeze before trying to pull away. He held on, pulling his arms more tightly around her and resting his cheek on top of her head. *Please don't leave me*, his body seemed to say. *Please.*

'Ade,' she said, soft but firm.

His arms fell away, and she stepped back, busying herself with the opened door so she didn't have to face him.

'You look beautiful,' he told her, even though she'd deliberately dressed as neutrally as possible. She'd spent hours deciding what to wear. Knew that if she dressed too casually, he'd think she didn't care, but if she overdressed, he'd think she was trying to impress him, to show him what he was missing, which was a lot closer to the truth than she cared to admit. And so, she'd opted for a pair of cream linen trousers with a sleeveless top, her hair piled on top of her head in her signature bun.

Ade, who clearly hadn't received the don't-overdo-it memo, was dressed in the suit she knew he only wore on special occasions – weddings, award ceremonies and, now, apparently, dinner at home with her.

'No jacket?' he asked.

'It's in the car.'

He tried and failed to hide his disappointment, and Cynthia realised that he probably thought it meant she had no intention of staying. Which, in a way, was true.

After she'd returned from Manchester the night before, she'd gone back to Mark's apartment. She'd thought things would be awkward between them, but as soon as she'd arrived, Mark had apologised again, explained that he had a vague memory of meeting Francis at one of Emma's work dos, and had got mad because he'd thought she'd heard that he was in town and was looking to cause trouble.

Honestly, she felt sorry for him. He'd apparently risked it all for love, and all he'd got in return was an ex-wife who wanted to ruin his life. She hoped when she and Ade broke up, they could at least be cordial, maybe even friends.

If they broke up, Cynthia corrected herself as she

followed Ade past the living room where the door was inexplicably shut.

'Something for later,' Ade told her, leading them into the kitchen, where he'd recreated the meal from their second date, when she'd taken him out for Jamaican food.

'I didn't think it would be a good idea to recreate the first one.' He chuckled and then winced. 'Sorry, I didn't think. Here.' He pulled a chair out for her and allowed her to sit before pushing it back in.

'Did you make all of this?' Cynthia asked, taking in the rice and peas and curry chicken.

He settled in the chair opposite her and placed a napkin on his lap. 'Yeah, mostly. I had a little help from Google. And Tayo.'

'It's good.' Not as good as the mac and cheese Mark had made for her, but still delicious. She was glad to hear that he and Tayo were getting along too. It meant she might not have to convince him to let him stay here if they decided to break up for good.

Their conversation remained frustratingly cordial. Ade asked her about her trip to Manchester and whether she'd managed to visit her parents. She replied that she had not, and Ade didn't press her for a reason or reprimand her for not making the most of the fact that both her parents were alive, well and together, something he always pointed out whenever her parents came up in conversation. She was a little disappointed that he hadn't said anything.

Instead, he listened as Cynthia told him about the movies she'd watched with Valerie, as well as Valerie and Frank's baby situation. She skipped over the part about her non-date with Mark.

There was a lengthy stretch of silence that probably lasted only a minute but felt like five. Cynthia wasn't a fan of this overly polite version of them.

'Dessert?' Ade asked.

'What are we having?'

Ade grinned, rose from his seat and bounced towards the kitchen door.

'Where are you going?'

'Just the living room,' he said, still grinning as he gestured for her to follow.

Oh lord, what was he up to? Cynthia dragged her feet as she followed behind him. And why was he so excited about it? He clearly didn't understand that their relationship was over. Which would make it even harder when she finally told him.

'Okay, close your eyes.'

'Ade—'

'Come on,' he said. 'Just this once.'

'Fine.' Cynthia closed her eyes, and a second later Ade's hand, warm and familiar, was in hers, pulling her into the living room.

'Okay, open them.'

'Oh, wow,' Cynthia said, once she'd followed his instructions.

There were cupcakes. About a dozen of them laid out on a folding table in the living room, all of them emblazoned with Ade and Cynthia's faces. They were cheesy, Cynthia could admit that, but it was just the kind of cheese that she liked, because it was Ade's cheese.

Cynthia went to choose one, but Ade stopped her.

'Can we talk first?' he asked, gesturing to the sofa. He took her hand in his and held it there.

'I'm sorry, Cynthia,' he said. Words he'd said a hundred and one times over the course of their relationship. 'I know I'm always apologising, but I really, truly mean it. I let my mother come between us when I promised you I wouldn't. I let her harm you when I was meant to be protecting you. I didn't stand up for you when I swore I'd always have your back. And I'm so sorry, babe, for all of it. I genuinely thought that she would come around, but I was wrong. I should have listened to you, should have known better. I know that doesn't mean much now, but I promise I'll do whatever it takes to fix this.'

Cynthia didn't know what to say. He'd obviously taken their time apart to reflect. She just wished he'd realised this *before* his mother tried to poison her.

'What are you thinking?' he asked when she was quiet for too long.

'I don't know,' she admitted. 'That I missed you, and—'

'I missed you, too.'

She shook her head. 'But I'm still so angry, Ade. Hurt, really. I—'

'I'm sorry. I never meant to hurt you.' If he interrupted her again, she was going to scream. And then leave.

'I know that. But you did. And you'll keep hurting me because you love your mother, and she hates me.'

It was really that simple, and Ade didn't try to patronise her by insisting otherwise.

'I'll never speak to her again if that's what you want. I'm as sick of her shit as you are.'

'I couldn't do that to you, Ade. And I can't keep putting myself through this.'

'I don't want her in my life anymore. Don't you get it? I'm choosing you.' And it had taken her almost dying for him to do it. The one thing she really needed him to do.

Ade stood up. 'Let's have some cake, okay?' he said. 'Take a breather.'

He handed her one of the cupcakes and took one for himself. Cynthia gazed at the faces smiling up at her. She couldn't remember when they had taken the photo, but they looked so happy. So unburdened.

He sat down next to her and waited.

'Well?' he said.

'Well, what?'

'Aren't you going to eat it?'

She looked down at the cake, then back at Ade.

'Later,' she told him. 'I think we should—'

'Please, just one bite,' he insisted. 'Then I promise we can talk about whatever you want.'

Cynthia sighed. 'Okay,' she said, tugging at the paper case then sinking her teeth into the cake. It was soft and creamy – and had an engagement ring sitting in the middle of it.

'For God's sake.'

Cynthia pulled it out, wiped it on a napkin and held it up to look at it.

'Is this . . . ?' Her voice caught in her throat, as she struggled to keep her heart from soaring.

'The exact same one.'

Around six months into their relationship, Ade had been looking to buy a new watch, and she'd gone with him to a family-run jeweller's in Battersea to get it.

Cynthia had no interest in watches, but the ring, with its silvery-blue gemstones, had caught her eye. Ade had seen her looking at it and asked her if it was something she could picture herself wearing. She'd shrugged and said it was okay, still in the phase where she was trying to play it cool, even though Ade had already told her he loved her.

'I went back the next day to get it for you because even then, six months in, I knew.'

Ade was on one knee now, and everything was moving

too fast. Thought after thought raced through Cynthia's mind so quickly she could barely decipher them. She needed to stop him before it was too late. Before she was forced to tear his heart apart.

'Ade, wait.'

There was panic in his eyes when he looked up at her. She gave him a reassuring smile even though she wanted to scream at him for being so stupid.

'Do you really think we're ready for this?' If she stayed calm, she might be able to salvage the situation without hurting him too badly. That was the last thing she wanted to do, and yet, why would he think proposing, today of all days, would be a good idea? They were in the middle of the worst fight they'd ever had. She'd basically broken up with him. If he knew her at all, the idea of proposing wouldn't have even crossed his mind.

Ade was rubbing his temples, his breathing heavy. 'I just know I want to spend the rest of my life with you.' He rested his hand on her knee. 'Everything else we can work out along the way.'

Cynthia covered his hand with her own. 'Now's not the time, Adz. We're not in a good place. Too much has happened, there are too many secrets.'

'I've never kept anything from you, babe.'

Cynthia sighed. Why did the men in her life keep lying to her?

'That first night Mama was here . . . I overheard the two of you talking.'

Ade dropped his hand from her leg. 'And?'

'And I heard you say something about telling Tayo the truth.'

'That has nothing to do with you, or us, or any of this.'

Cynthia shook her head in disbelief. 'What does she have on you?'

'It doesn't matter,' he said. '*She* doesn't matter anymore. It's just you and me now.'

'Not if you want us to get married. We can't keep secrets from each other, Ade. Especially not secrets about the woman who very recently tried to . . .' Cynthia squeezed her eyes shut and waited for the wave of anxiety to pass. It always came when she thought about what Mama had done, and it took her a few seconds for her breathing to settle.

'I'll never let her hurt you again, I swear.'

'Ade.'

'You don't understand.'

'Try me.'

Silence.

'I can't,' he finally said.

'Because I won't understand?' she asked.

'Because it doesn't matter,' he said firmly. 'Because I need you to trust me. To believe in us.'

Cynthia knew she couldn't do that. Not anymore. So she stood to her feet and held out the ring.

'I'm sorry, Ade,' she said. 'I love you. I really do, but I—'

'No, please.' Ade was on his feet now too. 'Okay,' he said. 'Okay.'

Cynthia thought he was going to sit back down, to tell her everything, but instead he walked right out of the room, leaving her standing there alone.

Seconds turned into minutes, and the silence grew heavy. If he didn't want to talk to her, then she wasn't going to wait around like the fool he'd let her become.

With that, she placed the ring on the coffee table and made her way to the back door, ready to leave the life they'd built behind.

'Where are you going?' Ade had returned. He was holding a small piece of paper in one hand, an amber-filled glass in the other.

His eyes went straight to the coffee table, disbelief then hurt flashing across his face.

'Ade, I didn't think you were . . .'

He held up his hand to stop her from speaking then closed his eyes as if he couldn't bear to look at her.

'Sit. Down,' he said, opening his eyes again but avoiding hers.

When she didn't move, he sighed in frustration.

'Sit down, Cynthia,' he said.

CHAPTER THIRTY-THREE

Ife, present day

'I was just looking for you,' Ife says, willing her heart to slow down so she can concentrate on getting out safely. She's already spotted what looks like the handle of a knife in the waistband of Mark's jeans.

'What are you doing here?'

'Oh, that,' Ife replies. 'I didn't see you at Cynthia's memorial and hadn't had a chance to respond to your messages. I wanted to check if you were okay. That's all.'

Something flickers beneath his anger, but he quickly conceals it.

'Don't play games, Ife.'

'I . . . I wasn't,' Ife insists. 'Like I said, I came to see you, found the door unlocked. When I saw the mess, I was worried. I thought something might have happened to you.'

Mark's expression softens into confusion. 'What do you mean?'

'Remember what I told you . . . about the break-ins? Cynthia's clothes. The photographs everywhere?' Ife gestures at the chaos in Mark's studio. 'It was exactly like this.'

Mark stares at her, waiting for her to get to the point.

'This is going to sound strange,' she says, 'but I think you were right . . . about something deeper going on.'

Mark scoffs.

Ife ignores him and instead focuses on steadying her hand as she fiddles in her pocket, silently praying she's remembered to bring it with her. 'I found this,' she says when she locates the key with the Afro girl key ring. 'I think it means something, but I don't even know what it's for. I thought maybe you might have an idea?'

Mark grabs the key and holds it up, lets the key ring dangle from the end, the girl swinging around in a circle.

'Do you know what it's for?' Ife asks again.

'Cynthia had a boat.'

'A boat?'

'Yeah.' Despite the circumstances, Mark's mouth kicks up into a nostalgic smile. 'She liked to sail. Loved it, really.' His frown returns. 'That must be how he drowned her.'

'You mean Ade?'

'I'm sorry, Ife . . . but—'

'No, it's fine,' Ife interrupts him, knowing that whatever she says next needs to be convincing. Her life might depend on it. 'I think you're right. Maybe it was an accident, maybe he didn't mean to, but . . . that's what Cynthia's been trying to tell me all along.'

Mark doesn't look like he believes her. 'Why the sudden change of heart?' he asks.

'I didn't want to believe it at first,' Ife says, her chest tightening. 'It's why I wasn't responding to your messages. But then, I remembered,' she continues. 'The night you said Cynthia disappeared . . . Ade came to see me.'

CHAPTER THIRTY-FOUR

One day before Cynthia's disappearance

'This is my father,' Ade said, showing her the scrap of paper which featured a man who looked so much like Tayo. They had the same handsome jawline, the same wide hopeful eyes. '*Was* my father.' He took a large gulp of the drink in his glass and swallowed.

'He wasn't a good man. Not at all,' he rushed on. 'Sometimes he'd come home from work after a bad day and just . . . lay into her. And then, the next morning, after he'd left, she'd lay into me.'

Cynthia put her hand on Ade's knee and squeezed, letting him know that she was there, that she was listening, but remaining silent.

'I was about six when it happened,' he continued. 'You have to understand that this had been going on for as long as I could remember. And I think . . . I don't know, maybe I just couldn't take it anymore.'

He looked at her to see if she understood, and Cynthia nodded, unsure of what to say, afraid of where his story was going.

'I woke up in the middle of the night and heard Mum

crying. She must have been a few months pregnant with Tayo, and for some stupid fucking reason, I decided to get out of bed . . . I still don't know why.

'We had this marble flooring all over the house. I used to love skating on it in my socks, and Mum would always say if I wasn't careful, I would crack my head open.

'And my dad, he was standing at the top of the stairs, and, I don't know.' He squeezed his eyes shut. 'There was so much blood. So much blood. Mum was *so* mad.' Cynthia clasped her hand over her mouth. 'She said I'd ruined their lives, that we'd never survive without him.'

'Ade . . .' Cynthia said, not wanting to believe what she was hearing, knowing that she needed to hear him say it. To feel the weight of what he'd done, of what the actions of an innocent little boy had ultimately done to them. 'Are you saying you killed him?'

'I didn't mean to,' he said, looking at Cynthia, his eyes begging her to believe him. 'Tayo doesn't even know about it,' he finished. 'He still thinks Dad was some kind of hero.' He took Cynthia's hand again. 'I know it's a lot. You don't have to say anything. God, it feels like someone just lifted the entire world off my shoulders.'

Cynthia's heart ached for the little boy who had been forced to endure a lifetime of shame, to live with a mother who used that shame to manipulate and control him. Who Ade was, his personality, his behaviour, made so much more sense now. Cynthia grabbed hold of him and held him tightly against her, wanting all the love she had for him, all the love he didn't get as a child, to somehow be transferred through her.

And then, she let go.

'I love you so much, Ade,' she said, knowing she needed to choose her next words more carefully than she'd ever chosen them before. 'You know I do. And I'm so sorry and sad and fucking *furious* that this happened to you. But' – she placed the ring in his palm and closed his fingers around it – 'I can't say yes. Not now, anyway. I need time to think.'

'So, you're not saying no,' he mused. 'Just . . . not yet?'

It was a cop-out, but Cynthia found herself nodding.

'Okay, then meet me at our spot tomorrow evening at six.' Ade handed her the ring. 'And keep this. Until you've made up your mind.'

Mark was making a stir-fry when Cynthia arrived back at the apartment. The smell of seasoned meat and onions filled the air.

'Did you do it?' he asked, the moment she stepped into the kitchen. He lifted the frying pan from the heat and shook it but didn't look up.

Ignoring his question, Cynthia grabbed a bottle of water from the fridge, chugged half of it down and settled on one of the kitchen stools, trying to make sense of what had just happened.

Ade had proposed to her. She had a ring in her pocket. But she'd said no, right? Cynthia closed her eyes and rested her head in her hands. She'd said *maybe*. She had gone over there to tell him their relationship was over, and now she was *maybe* engaged. Why hadn't she just said no? What the hell was wrong with her?

'Cynthia,' Mark placed the plate on the table in front of her and squeezed her shoulder, gently kneading his fingers into the muscle there.

'It's okay. Breakups are hard, but we . . . you'll get through it.'

Head still in one hand, Cynthia held up the ring with the other.

'Holy shit.'

Cynthia sighed.

'Are you crazy?' His voice had changed from concerned to angry, and Cynthia could feel herself getting angry as well.

'Don't start with me, Mark.'

'His mother tried to—'

'Mark.'

'Fine,' Mark took the stool next to her and stabbed a piece of beef with a fork. 'Psychopath mother aside. You can't marry him.'

Cynthia wanted to ask him why. Despite his flaws, Ade was still the love of her life, and that wasn't going to change any time soon, was it?

But beyond the anger, beyond the concern, Cynthia saw something else lingering in Mark's eyes. Something she couldn't name.

'Don't you think I know that?' she said. 'I just didn't want to hurt him, so I told him I'd think about it.'

'Jesus Christ.'

'Mark.' Cynthia sent him a warning glare.

'No, Cynthia. You listen to me. Marry him, don't marry him, whatever. But you can't lead him on. It'll only make things worse.'

'Okay,' Cynthia conceded. She didn't want to talk with him about this anymore. He didn't understand that some things were easier said than done. There was a beat of silence. Mark chewed his food, and Cynthia took a sip from her water bottle.

'How'd it go today?' she asked.

Mark's expression softened, and excitement danced in his eyes.

'The final meeting with the investors went well,' he said. 'They said they're looking forward to the show. And meeting you.'

'No way.'

'Yes way.'

'Urgh, Mark.' Cynthia got up and gave Mark a tight hug from behind. 'Thank you, thank you, thank you.'

'We still have some work to do. Your business plan is good, but your projections are a little off. We can work on it tonight, if you're up for it?'

'Yeah, of course. Still, thank you. For helping me get this far.'

They were both too giddy to work, and they eventually ended up on the living-room floor, with two bottles of wine between them, music playing in the background.

'Wait, is this the one from the car the other night?'

'Mmm,' he replied, his skin flushed. 'You like it?'

Cynthia bent her head to listen more closely. The lyrics, the melody, they had so much pain, so much longing. 'It's beautiful,' Cynthia said. 'Did you write it for Emma?'

Mark glared at her in a way that obviously meant no, and Cynthia giggled.

'I was just asking,' she said.

'Hey, don't you owe me a dance?' He put his glass down on the coffee table, rose to his feet and stretched his hand out to meet hers.

She knew he was trying to make up for the night at the club so she let him pull her from the floor, and they danced arm in arm, Mark holding her firmly against him.

As expected, he danced well, never missing a beat, always

spinning her at just the right moment. One song faded into another until they were both breathless.

A few strands of Cynthia's braid-out had escaped from her bun, and Mark gently tucked them away.

He lifted her chin so she was gazing up at him, leant his head forward and waited. She nodded, and he kissed her, slowly, tenderly, like he was savouring the moment, filing it away in his memory.

It was the first time she'd kissed anyone other than Ade in years, and it felt strange. Mark's lips were colder, more moist, his tongue more adventurous, his hands more needy. It felt good to feel wanted, even though her heart hurt so much, and Cynthia wondered if Mark was feeling the same way. If he too was using his lips to battle his demons.

It didn't matter, at least not now. Tonight, she didn't want to think about Ade, tonight she just wanted to be with Mark – simple, uncomplicated Mark, who, like her, was just trying to escape his pain.

Decision made, Cynthia deepened the kiss, pressing herself against him.

'Cynthia,' he breathed, watching her through soft-lidded eyes as she smiled up at him. 'God, you're so beautiful.' He kissed her again. 'I love you so much,' he whispered.

CHAPTER THIRTY-FIVE

Ife, present day

Ife lets the memory of Ade, drunk, upset, banging on her door, back into her mind after months of trying to suppress it.

She'd been in a rush to leave the house and hadn't wanted to let him in at first, but he'd pushed his way through.

'Uh, excuse you,' she'd said, rolling her eyes. She shut her front door with a sigh and was about to lay into him when she saw he'd been crying, the smell of rum exuding from his breath.

'Dey, what's wrong?'

'Nothing.' He pulled her into him, squeezing her against his chest so that she suddenly felt breathless. 'I've just missed you so much, Fey.' After Mama had told her about the crayfish incident, she'd been keeping her distance, but now she allowed herself to stay in his arms a moment too long before pulling away.

'Where's Cynthia?'

He shrugged, but Ife could see he was doing everything he could not to fall apart. 'She's gone.'

Ife's breath caught in her chest. 'What do you mean—'

'I . . . ended it with her. It's over—'

'And now you're drunk, and lonely, and looking for company. Haven't we played through this script enough times already, Ade? It's getting old.'

He insisted it wasn't like that this time, that yes, he'd had one or two drinks, but he hadn't been clearer about anything in his entire life. Ife was the one for him. He'd just been too stubborn to see it.

'What happened with Cynthia?'

'It doesn't matter.' He tried but failed to hide the obvious pain that flashed across his face.

'It matters to me.'

'She wasn't you.'

Ife made a face.

'It's true. You've always been there for me. Always had my back no matter what I've done. I know I don't deserve you. I know I haven't been a good friend to you.' He squeezed his eyes shut. 'But I need you, Fey. More than I need anything or anyone in this world.' He took her hands in his. 'I love you, Fey. I'm sorry it's taken me this long to realise it.'

He leant down to kiss her, but she stepped back. Of course, she wanted to believe him, had spent years waiting to hear these very words. But she also knew Ade, knew how fickle his feelings for her could be. What if he woke up tomorrow and he changed his mind? She would have jeopardised everything for what was basically, at least in Ade's eyes, a one-night stand.

'I'm seeing someone,' she told him.

'And you love him?'

'That's not the point, Ade.'

'Then what *is* the point, Fey?'

'You can't keep using me as your rebound girl.'

'I don't . . .'

She shot him a daggered glare.

'Okay, then marry me.'

Ife laughed. 'You're kidding.'

'I've never been more serious about anything in my life. I love you, and, despite the look you're giving me right now, I know you love me. So, why waste any more time?'

'Because . . . Cynthia!'

Ade huffed. 'I don't know what you want from me.'

'I want you to be sure,' she whispered. 'Come back in two weeks, when you're sober and not . . . hurting so much.'

'So, if I propose in two weeks' time, you'll say yes?'

'Maybe.'

He called her every day for the following two weeks. They had long, soul-deep conversations that continued over text, and Ife found herself falling for him in a completely new way. She knew deep down it was wrong, but she couldn't help it.

When day fourteen arrived, he phoned her up at midnight and asked if she was ready.

'Go on then,' she told him.

'Fey.'

'Yeah?'

'Will you . . . actually, hold on a sec.'

There was a rustle, and then the phone went silent.

'Fey, you there?'

'Yep.'

'Good.'

Her doorbell rang, and Ife let out an exasperated sigh.

'Hang on.'

She opened the door, and when she looked down, she found Ade on one knee, an opened ring box in his hands.

'I wanted you to know that I meant it.'

Up until their wedding day, until Ade's arrest, Ife had clung to his words, had let herself believe them.

But now, as she says all this to Mark, she's forced to reckon with the fact that maybe, just maybe, Ade had lied to her that night. That maybe he *had* been using her all this time. That she's married a man who not only doesn't love her but might also be a murderer.

'Like I said,' she tells Mark. 'I didn't want to believe it, but when I think about everything that's happened, it's the only thing that makes sense.'

'Do you really believe that?' Ade asks, stepping into the room.

CHAPTER THIRTY-SIX

The day of Cynthia's disappearance

Cynthia couldn't sleep. Although Mark had tried to downplay his declaration of love, claiming he'd just been caught up in the moment, it didn't make sense.

Sure, they'd become good friends over the past few months, and he'd been so supportive when she'd needed it, but that didn't equate to love, did it? Not in the way that Mark meant.

And he'd meant it. She could tell from the way his eyes had lingered on hers, the expectant smile that had played on his lips like he was waiting for her to say it back.

But it didn't make sense.

Mark was in love with someone else. Had uprooted his entire life for this woman he refused to tell her about. There was no way he could be in love with them both.

Unless . . .

No no no no no. No.

Cynthia cast her mind back, replaying her friendship with Mark in her head. The way he just seemed to *know* her – her favourite food, the type of music she liked, the fact that she used to go to church. He was also so damn caring

– too caring – about someone he'd just met: going out of his way to do things for her, like speaking to the investors or getting genuinely furious at the way Ade had been treating her. Who would do all that for someone they'd just met if they weren't in love with them?

Nah, Mark was just weird, Cynthia told herself, pulling her duvet over her head, even though all the lights were already off. He was probably just projecting his feelings for this other woman onto her. He probably felt embarrassed about the whole thing.

She closed her eyes, and Francis's confused expression when he saw the two of them together popped into her mind. Mark's hasty exit and his fury at her questioning. That couldn't be explained away so easily, and Cynthia wasn't sure if Francis had been shocked because she should have realised he and Francis knew each other, or was just surprised to see his ex-girlfriend with someone he knew.

The name thing was strange, though. Except people changed and swapped their names all the time, didn't they?

Cynthia sighed and pulled her phone from its charger. She didn't usually like to google people she knew, it felt like an invasion of their privacy, but on this one occasion it was warranted. So, she typed Mark Nelson into the search bar and scrolled through the results.

His LinkedIn profile and website for his music appeared,

but apart from that, there wasn't much else. Just a bunch of social-media profiles that didn't seem to belong to him.

She tried Christopher Nelson next and got a few hits on the Companies House website. Mark's music production company was listed under this name, as well as a property business, the studio listed as its address.

Cynthia's stomach tightened. If she was understanding this correctly, Mark owned the building she was sleeping in right now. So why had he told her that he was renting the apartment? Or maybe he hadn't said those exact words. She tried to remember what he'd said the day they met. Something about needing a place to stay and Janine saying it was okay. Either way, he'd lied to her, just like he'd lied to her in Manchester.

She closed the website and opened her Instagram to fish out the message he or someone in his company had sent her about renting out the studio.

They'd simply given her an email address to organise a viewing, and Janine had handled it from there.

She clicked on the person's profile, but it was private and she hadn't followed them.

Cynthia scrolled through some of her posts from around that time to see if the profile had interacted with any of them. They had liked several of her posts that year – and in the many years prior. If this *was* Mark, he'd been following her for a long time. As sick as this made her feel, she knew she needed more than this if she was going to confront Mark about it.

By the next morning, she'd changed her mind about confronting Mark. If he really was pretending to be someone else, trying to talk to him about it would be futile, and potentially dangerous.

Instead, she hid in her room, hoping to hear his footsteps leaving the apartment.

He came knocking at around half past eleven. At first, Cynthia didn't answer the door, but he kept on hounding her, saying he knew she was avoiding him but could they please just talk?

Cynthia pulled on her dressing gown and opened the door, blocking his entry to her room. The fact that he'd lied to her about the studio, and who knew what else, made her feel both furious and ill.

'Look, I said I'm sorry, okay,' he told her. 'It was a stupid thing to say, and a silly joke to make. If I knew it would freak you out so much, I wouldn't have said it.'

'It's fine,' Cynthia said, although she couldn't quite bring herself to smile at him. 'I just need a bit of space, that's all.'

After shutting the door on Mark, Cynthia dived back under her covers and scoured the Internet for more information about who he really was, but very little else came up. She tried to distract herself by watching dance videos while half listening to Mark as he moved around the apartment.

After what felt like hours, she finally heard the front door close, and waited for a few minutes before throwing her duvet away from her and getting out of bed to begin her search.

She went to Mark's bedroom first, rifled through his drawers and his wardrobe to see if she could find anything, but there was nothing incriminating and she wasn't even sure what she was looking for.

She tried the kitchen next, and even the bathroom, until finally she found herself outside a smaller room which Cynthia had presumed was off-limits because Mark hadn't showed it to her when he'd given her an apartment tour.

If it had been anyone other than Mark, she would have expected the door to be locked, but he didn't even lock the door when he went to the bathroom or left the apartment, so all she had to do was turn the handle.

She wasn't sure why she was surprised to find that it was Mark's home music studio, kitted out with what looked like expensive gear. Resisting the urge to play with it, she went through Mark's drawers and at first found nothing except old CDs and notebooks with song lyrics and chords. Finally, she came to the last drawer and found the contract she'd signed to rent the studio, the name of his company listed at the top. This at least confirmed her suspicions about Mark already knowing who she was when they met. But it didn't explain much else.

Just as Cynthia was about to leave, she spotted a built-in cupboard at the back of the room. She hadn't noticed it before because the door was painted the same dark blue as the walls. With a sense of dread, Cynthia opened its doors to find at least a dozen boxes of varying sizes.

Heart racing, Cynthia took one out.

Inside were photographs of her.

They looked professional, some of them showing the highlights of her career. Cynthia wasn't sure if Mark had taken them himself or had downloaded them from the Internet and had them printed.

Her question was answered when she found several ticket stubs from her performances. They were nestled in amongst clippings from newspapers and magazines, her name circled in rose gold.

Feeling nauseous, Cynthia pulled out another box from the cupboard. This one had pictures of her and Ade, some taken from afar, some from online. Several with Ade's face crossed out with a neatly drawn X.

Just about ready to throw up, Cynthia opened yet another box. The blurry photos of her and Francis almost made her pass out. It also held several years of their church's newsletter, with pictures of her on the front page, little hearts drawn around her face.

So Mark had attended her father's church? How had she not known this? Of course, it had thousands of congregants, so there was no way she could know everyone. But Francis had known who he was, so why hadn't she?

Not wanting to continue but unable to stop, Cynthia pulled out one of the larger boxes at the bottom of the cupboard. Inside were leather-covered journals that seemed to have been written over several years.

She flicked through them, and sentences jumped out at her.

Why does Francis get to have her and I don't?
God I love her so much it hurts. One day, Cynthia, one day.
Today I told her father about Francis.
She's with this new guy Ade. He seems like a right prick.

Cynthia slammed the last journal shut, unable to take any more. She was numb with shock, unsure of what to do next.

Put this shit away and then get the hell out of here.

Cynthia nodded and piled everything into different boxes, too dizzy to reorganise them into the ones she'd found them in, and pushed them back into the cupboard.

She ran to her room, dragged her suitcase from under the bed and stuffed it with as many of her clothes as she could manage, her fuzzy mind racing for what to do next. She would have to cancel her classes, find somewhere else to stay.

And then she heard it.

A door gently closing.

Quiet footsteps creeping on carpet.

She froze. Covered her mouth to keep herself from sobbing.

It can't be him. It can't.

CHAPTER THIRTY-SEVEN

Ife, present day

'Dey... I...' Ife looks at him with pleading eyes, trying to communicate the danger they're both in. Instead, he stalks towards her, his eyes, hurt and betrayed, fixed on hers.

She glances at Tayo, who looks both solemn and afraid. Like he isn't sure what his brother is going to do. Ade comes to a stop a few inches away from her. She leans back on Mark's desk to create space between them.

Ade laughs. It is short and sad.

'What, so you're afraid of me now?' he says. 'One conversation with him and suddenly I'm dangerous?'

'Wait, you didn't tell him?' Mark is smiling a disbelieving smile.

Ade continues to stare her down, and she swallows, suddenly feeling light-headed, overwhelmed by the three men who have formed a circle around her.

'Tell me what?'

'Nothing.' Ife shakes her head, ignoring the pounding in her throat. 'Let's just go.' She tries to push past them towards the door, but Mark is quicker than she is, and he slams it shut, locking them inside.

Panic flashes across Tayo's face, and she knows he too has seen the knife.

Ade still hasn't moved, is still waiting for her response.

'Tell me what?' he asks again.

'That she came to see me ages ago,' Mark says when Ife doesn't answer. 'That she thought that the police were right to arrest you.'

'Fey?'

Ife's shaking her head, but for some reason she can't seem to defend herself. Isn't sure she wants to.

Ife, please let me in.

'I told her what you did,' Mark continues. 'How you proposed to Cynthia and she rejected you. How much you hated the fact that we were living together. That that was why you did what you did.'

'Ife?'

Okay, then marry me.

'I gave her Cynthia's ring too. That's all she really needed in the end, to know what a lying, murdering piece of shit you really are.'

I wanted you to know that I meant it.

'Cynthia deserved so much better than you. I knew it, she knew it, and now' – he nods towards Ife – 'your wife knows it too.'

Ade is at Mark's throat now, pinning him to the door with his arm, calling him a liar over and over again, telling him to take it back. Mark tries and fails to break free, his face turning red from the effort.

Ife knows she should do something, say anything to calm him down, to stop the chaos. But she is frozen. Images of her and Ade and Cynthia and Mark swirl in her mind. She does not know if Mark is telling the truth, only that there is something more than jealousy between them. That Ade has lied to her, about almost everything.

Tayo, then, steps in, pulling Ade by his hood, telling him to *leave it man, it isn't worth it.* Somehow, he manages to get him off Mark, and Ade's eyes, red with tears, meet hers. Mark takes this moment to shove Ade into Ife and Ife into the table. Ade's reaction, a punch in the face, is instant, and Mark stumbles backwards, then hits him back.

They push and shove until both of them are on the floor. Tayo tries to separate them and ends up in the tussle.

A flash of silver, a squeal, silence. Blood drains onto the carpet. Ife covers her mouth, afraid that Ade has been hurt, conflicted because either he or Mark must have hurt Cynthia. She is sure of it now.

Ade rises to his feet. Tayo, still on the floor, removes his jumper and presses it into Mark's leg.

'Fey,' Ade says, limping towards her. 'Did he hurt you?'

Ife takes a step back. And then another one. She realises now that it's truly over between them. That she will be raising her baby alone.

She slips her hand into her pocket and is not surprised to feel a warm metal object resting against her fingers. She closes her eyes and releases a sad sigh.

Finally, she pulls her phone from her pocket and dials 999.

CHAPTER THIRTY-EIGHT

The day of Cynthia's disappearance

Cynthia stood frozen for one long gut-wrenching moment.

Listening.

Waiting.

Silently praying.

When the moment had passed, she inched towards the door, pressing her ear against it.

She waited, listened, prayed. When there was only silence, she gently opened the door and peeked to see if anyone was there.

No Mark.

Wasting no more time, she grabbed her suitcase and her bag and made a dash across the living room to the front door. For one horrifying second, her hands were too shaky to unlock it. But then it opened, and she was free.

Finally outside, Cynthia rummaged through her bag in search of her car keys. Nothing. And her car was not where she'd parked it. He must have taken it. Must have known that she would run from him.

Hidden in the alleyway behind Nyara's café, she allowed herself a moment to think. She considered going to the police or asking Nyara for help, but she could see through the window that the café was packed, and, besides, what would she say? How could she possibly explain this situation without sounding insane?

Ade, a voice in her head said. *Go to Ade.* She glanced down at her watch. They were meant to be meeting in less than half an hour.

She didn't know how she was going to explain all this to him, how she was going to admit that he'd been right all along.

He would want her to move back in with him, to accept his proposal, but . . .

Oh no. No no no.

Cynthia squeezed her eyes shut. Patted her jacket, her trouser pockets, searched through her bag to find the ring, but she knew she didn't have it. Knew she'd left it nestled in her top drawer, out of sight, out of mind.

She gazed across the street but knew it was too late to go back. Mark could return at any moment. She needed to go. *Now.*

She wound her way around the back of Nyara's café and followed a path to the foot of the hill. On the other side was a cliff, the beach and the sea just beyond. Dragging her suitcase behind her, she climbed until she reached the top, adrenalin surging her forward even when her aching legs urged her to stop.

At the top, in the spot she and Ade had sat countless times, legs dangling carelessly over the edge, a hooded figure was waiting for her.

'Cynthia,' Mark said, pulling his hood down and moving towards her. She took several steps back, afraid of what he might do. His eyes were red, his hair wild, and he looked like he'd been crying. 'Please, don't look at me like that. Just . . . let me explain, okay?'

He was coming closer again, and Cynthia circled away from him, her back now facing the cliff's edge.

'Hey.' He grabbed hold of her hand, and it took all Cynthia's strength not to snatch it back. She wasn't sure what he would do if she tried to escape. Besides, Ade would be here any minute now to help her. Any minute now.

'I know it looks bad. But it's not how it seems. It's just . . . I've always liked you. And when I found out you moved to Windchapel, I realised it was our chance to finally be together.'

'You stalked me for *years*. Changed your name. *Tricked* me into moving in with you—'

'No, no.' He shook his head, his voice raising several octaves. 'I was just . . . keeping an eye on you, making sure you were okay. And that kiss . . .'

Cynthia winced. 'Mark—'

'Nothing's changed, not really. I'm still me. I'm still the

guy you were falling for.' He grinned through his tears. 'Just give me another chance, okay? Give *us* a chance.'

He pulled her into him, and Cynthia closed her eyes, her body a rag doll as she waited for him to let her go.

'I'm sorry, okay.' He sniffed. 'We'll work this out.'

'Is this some kind of joke?'

Cynthia's eyes flew open at the sound of Ade's voice. Mark at last released her, but instead of walking away, he took her hand in his, gripping it more tightly when she tried to break free.

'I can't believe this,' he said. 'I poured my heart out, gave you all the space you asked for, and in return you bring *him* – for what, protection?'

'No, Ade, I didn't—'

Cynthia tried to go to him, but Mark refused to let her.

'Oh, wow.' Ade looked from her to Mark but was obviously too hurt or angry or stubborn to see Mark's wild eyes, Cynthia's distress. 'I'm such an idiot. I *knew* something was going on between you two. *Knew* I shouldn't have listened when you said you were just friends.'

'Please, just listen. We're not—'

'Nah, fuck you, Cynthia.' Ade shook his head in disgust. 'I'm done with this.'

Ade turned around and began to walk away.

'Ade, please just wait.' Cynthia tugged as hard as she could, but Mark was stronger than he looked.

'Yeah, walk away,' he said. 'She's better off without you. Wouldn't want her to end up like your father, would we?'

Ade froze. Turned again to face them.

'Say that again,' he said, taking a step forward, his eyes trained on Mark.

Mark dropped Cynthia's hand, and she immediately moved away from him. She wanted to go to Ade, but Mark took a step towards him so that they were almost touching.

'You heard me.'

Ade turned to Cynthia in disbelief.

'Yeah, she told me.'

'No, Ade, I didn't. I swear. He's been stalking me all this time.'

But Ade wasn't listening.

'Say it again,' he said, shoving Mark backwards. Mark stumbled but managed to right himself.

'I said' – he pushed Ade back – 'you don't deserve her.'

Ade pushed Mark again. Mark shoved Ade back. Cynthia stood there, confused that these two idiots were fighting over her, even though, right now, she didn't want either of them. Push, shove, push, shove, push, shove, on they went until Cynthia couldn't take it anymore, not when they were so close to the cliff's edge.

'Will you both stop?!' she shouted, trying to pull them apart but feeling helpless.

They pushed her out of the way, one of their arms connected with her chest, and she stumbled.

She tried to right herself, but her feet gave way, leaving her to free-fall backwards over the edge.

CHAPTER THIRTY-NINE

Cynthia's head hurts.

It isn't the take a couple of paracetamols and have a nap kind of headache. It feels as if someone is trying to pull her skull out through her nose. But she's going to be okay.

Any moment now, Ade will be running towards her to take her to the hospital.

She'll be in pain for a few hours, or a few days, or a few weeks. But then everything will be okay.

Somewhere in the distance, the chapel bell rings, signalling the start of the hour.

Footsteps. Light and quick at first, and then slow, heavy, cautious.

Trainers – hot pink, white stripes, three diamantés on the arch – slip into her line of vision.

She knows these trainers. Had hated them once. But they mean something different now. They mean hope.

'Oh my God. Oh my God,' she's saying. 'Cynthia, can you hear me?'

Yes, she says, but the words don't come out. She can barely breathe, let alone talk.

Her saviour reaches over to touch the side of her neck. Her hands are warm, gentle.

'Shit,' she says. Ade had told her that she very rarely swore, but now is as good a time as any.

'What happened? Did you fall?'

Cynthia imagines her looking up at the cliff, searching for answers.

'It's okay,' she says. 'You'll be okay.'

Footsteps, soft and light, except this time they are moving away from her.

'No, don't go.' In her desperation, Cynthia manages a gurgle.

But no one answers, and the footsteps are long gone now.

She's gone to get help, Cynthia tells herself.

She's coming back.

Any minute now.

ACKNOWLEDGEMENTS

To the incredible Kemi Ogunsanwo, thank you for believing in me and this story even before I really knew what it was, or what it could become. Thank you for your patience, your wisdom and your unrelenting support. I couldn't have asked for a better agent.

To my editor, Lochlann Binney, your enthusiasm for this book has completely blown me away. Thank you for your guidance, your openness, and for helping me become a better writer. It's been such a pleasure working with you.

To Phoebe Williams, Hannah Turner, Joanna Harwood, and the entire team at Faber, thank you for the time and energy you've put into bringing this book to life.

To Lottie Fyfe, thank you for your keen eye and spot-on insights.

To my writing group, Anna, Dacy, Jo, Ellen, Mei, and Maura, and to my supervisor Steven J Fowler, thank you all for your feedback and advice.

To Mum, Dad, Tobi Dipeolu, Gbemisola Okoye, Taiwo Dipeolu, Kitan Nathan-Marsh, Aunty Peri, Uncle Kunle, Omowunmi Dipeolu, Michael Okoye, Hayley Fairweather,

Victoria Kirby, Ifeoluwa Adeniyi, Fizza Imam, Sam Spedding, Kaleish Frankin, and Colette Passee, thank you for your continued support and encouragement.

To Jacob Mager and Abbas Mustafa, thank you for the thought-provoking conversation, the day-long writing sessions, and for reading the early drafts of this book countless times. I'm truly blessed to have such great friends.